PRAISE FOR JC

Or Else

"Hart remains a suspense writer to watch."

—*Publishers Weekly*

"*Or Else* is a thriller/suspense tour de force. Joe Hart has knocked it out of the park with a start-to-finish roller coaster ride of perfectly executed twists and expertly timed chills. Deep character development and rich narrative seals *Or Else*'s place as the not-to-be-missed domestic thriller/suspense of the year."

—Steven Konkoly, author of the Ryan Decker series and *Deep Sleep*

"The perfect thriller for a rainy afternoon, *Or Else* draws you into a web of small town secrets, lies, and intrigue and doesn't let you go. Hart's well-rendered setting and characters resonate like people and places you've known. Loved every minute of this absolute page-turner!"

—D. M. Pulley, bestselling author of *The Dead Key*

"Joe Hart has written compelling stories before, but it's in *Or Else* that he shows off just how good he is. This book checks all the boxes for me: a (seemingly) quiet, small-town drama—filled with those little quirks and secrets nobody wants to talk about—that quickly blossoms into something big, sinister, and menacing. Hart doesn't pull any punches on some serious issues, either: love, infidelity, family conflict . . . there's plenty to think about right up to the explosive ending. This is the thriller you'll be recommending for the foreseeable future."

—Matthew Iden, author of the Marty Singer series and *The Winter Over*

Obscura

"Joe Hart is a tremendous talent, and with *Obscura*, he has taken his storytelling to the next level. This is a genius work of science fiction, brimming with thrills, scares, and most importantly, heart. I devoured this book, and you will too."
—Blake Crouch, *New York Times* bestselling author of *Dark Matter* and the Wayward Pines series

"Outstanding . . . Fans of Blake Crouch's Wayward Pines series, with its combination of mystery, horror, and science fiction, will find this right up their alley."
—*Publishers Weekly* (starred review)

"This gripping book will be a must-read for fans of SF-based mysteries such as John Scalzi's *Lock In* and Kristine Kathryn Rusch's Retrieval Artist series, as well as aficionados of stories about science gone wrong, too far, or both."
—*Library Journal* (starred review)

"The pacing is excellent from beginning to end."
—*Los Angeles Times*

"Those seeking an off-planet sci-fi thriller with a haunting plotline will devour Joe Hart's *Obscura*, which reads quick and is jam-packed with terrifying surprises."
—The Real Book Spy

"For the reader who likes hard science fiction with some mystery and suspense thrown in, *Obscura* should hit the spot. It's not merely sci-fi, but a thriller wrapped in the deadly solitude of space with a determined heroine who refuses to give up."
—*New York Journal of Books*

WHERE THEY LIE

ALSO BY JOE HART

The Dominion Trilogy

The Last Girl
The Final Trade
The First City

The Liam Dempsey Mysteries

The River Is Dark
The Night Is Deep

Novels

Lineage
Singularity
EverFall
The Waiting
Widow Town
Cruel World
Obscura
I'll Bring You Back
We Sang in the Dark
Or Else

Novellas

Leave the Living

Short Story Collections

Midnight Paths: A Collection of Dark Horror
Something Came Through: And Other Stories

Short Stories

"The Line Unseen"
"Outpost"
"And The Sea Called Her Name"
"The Exorcism of Sara May"

Comics

The Last Sacrifice

WHERE THEY LIE

A THRILLER

JOE HART

THOMAS & MERCER

Published by Thomas & Mercer, Seattle

www.apub.com

Amazon, the Amazon logo, and Thomas & Mercer are trademarks of Amazon.com, Inc., or its affiliates.

ISBN-13: 9781662508080 (paperback)
ISBN-13: 9781662508097 (digital)

Cover design by Shasti O'Leary Soudant

Cover image: © Magdalena Anna Kocjan / Arcangel; © Igor Vitkovskiy / Shutterstock

Printed in the United States of America

To the readers everywhere.

No lie ever reaches old age.

—Sophocles

1

"Come on, Dooly, just sit down, for God's sake. You're gonna fall overboard."

Roger watched his goofy adolescent shepherd meander across the small deck of the sailboat and turn in a circle. He sniffed a neat coil of rope and chuffed once before pacing back to Roger's side, giving the darkened entry to the cabin a wary look.

"We're going down there soon, you know," Roger said, double-checking the angle of the jib. "That or we'll have to grow gills."

The sea was choppy, a wind out of the northwest pushing them along at a steady five knots. Banks of low clouds churned off the port, and dark curtains of rain draped across the Pacific in the distance. Two miles in the opposite direction, the shoreline floated like a mirage, the land rising up in the suggestion of foothills and mountains beyond. Farther south, angles of sunlight cut through the cloud cover, and Roger looked longingly back, wondering if they should turn around.

It was the first overnight trip he'd taken since acquiring the boat six months ago. For the past year, after discovering an unknown love of sailing, he'd kept to short day trips, traveling only to ports reachable in a few hours, always keen not to push the hobby into foolishly dangerous territory. He was meticulous in his planning and skittish when it came to taking chances, so the unanticipated storm made him deeply uneasy.

Roger checked the instrumentation again. Four hours to their destination and no sufficient docking nearby. Dooly whined nervously, and Roger stroked the shepherd's head. "Don't worry, bud. Worst comes to worst I'll find us a bay we can anchor in." Dooly looked at him with the same amount of comfort Roger felt from the reassurance.

A spate of rain hissed across the boat, there and gone like a lashing, and Roger was about to pick Dooly up and carry him below no matter how much he hated it down there when the dog's ears pricked up. Roger frowned, following the shepherd's sudden intent stare toward land.

A small plane had dropped out of the clouds and was descending toward them.

It was far enough away for its details to be obscured by the gray morning but close enough for Roger to know something was wrong. Without taking his eyes off the plane, he pawed at the gunwale until his fingers closed over a pair of binoculars. He put them up to his face as more rain pattered across the deck.

The plane was a single engine, its prop a black whir in front of the cockpit. For a moment it continued a steep descent, and Roger's jaw loosened. It was going to hit the water. He was going to watch it plummet straight into the waves, but he couldn't get himself to look away. Just as he was sure it was past the point of no return, a blur of movement came from behind the windshield—two shapes struggling in the front seats.

The wingtips yawed, and the plane banked hard to the right, turning in a wide arc while continuing its downward slant. The sound of its engine was clear now, a flat blatting with a whining rpm undertone.

The plane's flaps jumped, and gradually it gained a measure of altitude. Roger's chest loosened—a fleeting sense that all would be well—then the plane tipped sideways again and lurched in their direction.

As if in a dream, Roger lowered the binoculars, squinting against the rain. For a second everything was crystalline. He was aware of

Dooly's fur pressed into his side and the warmth of his body—how the dog was shivering.

Each whitecap pronounced in rolling foam.

Every raindrop dimpling the water's surface.

His breath pluming in the cool air.

Then the plane dropped lower, coming straight and fast as a bullet, and Roger knew it was going to hit them. All the wide, wide Pacific to crash in, and the damn thing was going to hit their boat. The absurdity of it temporarily froze him in place. He had time to think he was going to die without ever making partner at the firm or finally getting the nerve up to ask for the number of the pretty barista who had been flirting with him for the last month before grasping Dooly around his midsection and diving toward the cabin stairs.

There was a cacophony of sound as the plane cruised lower and the two of them landed at the bottom of the steps in a heap. Dooly yelped and Roger grunted as something sharp raked his side. For a second he had a clear view up the cabin stairs, and he caught the flash of the plane's belly, close enough to make out individual streaks of oil on the white paint. Roger hugged his dog, trying to keep Dooly tight to his own body, knowing any second there would be the crushing weight of unforgiving metal tearing into his flesh and bones, then endless sprawling pain.

The plane's howl was the only sound in the world. Then it relented, growing fainter with each heartbeat thundering through Roger's chest and vision.

It missed them. They were still alive.

He let go of Dooly, and the dog skittered away to the far end of the cabin as Roger climbed up the steps on all fours back into the open air.

The plane had regained some altitude but continued to tilt drunkenly one way, then the other. Roger scrambled for his binoculars, which had fallen dangerously close to the boat's edge, and jammed them to his eyes.

The aircraft rose once more, a bird catching a powerful updraft, and then it banked hard to the right and angled down irreversibly. It seemed to hang there for a split second, an image of its bulk suspended over the expanse of rough sea forever seared into Roger's mind, before plummeting through a swath of rain into the ocean. A spume of water cascaded up silently in the distance and fell, the rough sea resuming its indifferent rolling.

"Oh God, oh no," he said, letting the binocs drop from his face. His stomach sloshed with acid, and he wondered in a detached way if he was going to be sick.

Roger stumbled to the small alcove where the deck radio was positioned, grabbing the mic from its hook. And even as he began to hail the coast guard over and over in a voice unrecognizable to his own ears, all he could see was the small pale face that had been pressed against the rear passenger window of the plane's fuselage before it had banked the last time.

A child, he thought, saying, "Mayday, Mayday, Mayday," into the rain-flecked handset.

There'd been a kid on the plane.

2

I know there will be a morning when I wake up and don't think of my brother. But it's not today. I don't know when that day will come, or if I want it to. What does it say about us when we begin to accept someone else's sacrifice? When we begin to forget. Is it natural, the way things should be, all ordained and right in the flow of life? Or is it a betrayal to their memory? An injustice.

I don't know. I really don't know.

———

He was there now as I hurried through the rain to the low house ahead. Paul. His face was beginning to blur around the edges as time ate away at memory, but it was as if his arms were around me like the very last time I saw him alive. He'd always had a way of making me feel safe and stronger than I was, and I leaned into that feeling now. I'd need it soon enough.

The officer accompanying me climbed out of his cruiser, and we nodded at one another while stepping into the shelter of the porch. I rang the doorbell and shook the rain from my hair.

Footsteps approached on the other side of the door, and there was a pause where I knew we were being inspected through the peephole, then a dead bolt twisted, and a woman's face appeared in the door's gap.

"Yeah?" Anita Warren was thin and pale and had the strung-out look of someone either running on no sleep, drugs, or both.

"Mrs. Warren, I'm Nora McTavish with state child services." I had my ID ready and showed it to her. She gave it a cursory glance, then stared blankly at me. "May we come in?"

"If I say no?"

"We have a warrant. The officer will have to use force to gain entry," I said, disliking how the words tasted. Anita seemed to weigh her options, then slung the door wide and retreated deeper into the house.

The interior was narrower than the outside suggested, the space divided into miniature caricatures of rooms. Here was the abbreviated kitchen piled high with dishes waiting to be cleaned, unopened mail spilling off a table onto linoleum so ugly it had to be intentional. Farther back the kitchen emptied into a bathroom, where someone had miscalculated how big the vanity was as it stopped the swing of the door from opening all the way. To the left, through a halfhearted arch, a living room ended abruptly in a sectional couch, which engulfed the space. And sitting on the couch were the two reasons I was here.

A boy and a girl, Bobby and Amanda—nine and seven. They were looking at me like I might be some sort of addition to whatever mind-numbing cartoon spilled from the TV before them. Bobby stared at me long after his sister returned her attention to the screen. Maybe he knew why I was here.

I hated this.

"It's their father. He cuffs them around once in a while when they won't listen," Anita said. She'd found a glass half full of some amber liquid and was leaning against the countertop, shifting her eyes from me to the deputy like she was unsure of who to talk to. "Hits me, too, but you aren't here for me, are you?"

"If you'd like to file a complaint with the deputy, he'd be happy to take your statement. I can put you in touch with someone from social services too. They'd—"

"Oh yeah, sure," Anita said, cutting me off. She took a slug of her drink and set it down. "That'll do me a whole lot of good when he comes home in the middle of the night drunk off his ass. Just drop your paperwork on the table and go."

"Mrs. Warren, you didn't appear in court for your scheduled hearing."

"When was this?"

"Yesterday. You were sent a summons in the mail."

"Didn't get it."

I watched her take another sip of whatever was in the glass. Maybe she hadn't gotten the summons; it happened. More likely it was in the pile of mail on the table, unopened or shredded and tossed to the side—just another request in an already tumultuous life. Except nothing would be the same after this.

I licked my lips. They were dry. My heart kicked at my ribs. I'd never gotten used to this.

I would never get used to this.

The papers were in my hand, and I didn't recall opening my briefcase. I held them out, feeling a tremor trying to make its way down my arm. "Mrs. Warren, this is a petition of temporary removal signed by a judge." A pause, and it felt like the tiny house had gotten even smaller. "I'll need Bobby and Amanda to come with me."

Those moments of suspension.

Before the reality hit. The half second before pain registered when you sliced yourself with a knife. Stepping off a stair expecting the floor and finding nothing but empty air.

Anita blinked. Her face changed. The little color in her cheeks drained, and she started shaking her head. No. No, no, no.

"No, no way," she said, words finally catching up with her motions. "You aren't taking my kids."

"I'm sorry. It's temporary, and you can make an appeal in court on the date listed." I tried holding the documents out farther, willing her to take them, like it would make it all better somehow. Something shifted in her eyes. A decision being made. "Anita . . ." I started, but that was when she lunged at me.

Her hands were reaching, not for the papers, but for my throat. I took a step back, and it was enough for the deputy to step in between us and grasp Anita's wrists, pulling her up short.

"Ma'am," he said quietly.

"No! You're not taking them! You're not taking my fucking kids!"

Anita whipsawed, trying to break loose from the deputy's grip, and there was something in the movement, some innate language that made my throat close up. It was a mother fighting for her children, knowing there would be consequences but not caring. I reached out to do something—comfort? Reassure? But a coldness inside me stilled my hand. It kept me blank and professional and allowed me to do what had to be done. To do my job.

The deputy nodded over one shoulder while Anita cried out for him to let her go, goddamn it.

In the living room the kids had quit watching TV. Their eyes were huge in their little faces, watching their mother throw her meager weight against the deputy. I knelt in front of them.

"Hi, my name is Nora. You're Bobby and Amanda, right?" I kept my voice low and steady, loud enough to be heard over their mother's shouts. They looked at me with the same blank expressions as they had while watching TV. "I know this is scary, but I'm here to take you both on a little trip. Does that sound okay?"

"Get out of my house!" Anita made another lunge, and the deputy finally pivoted, using her momentum to take her down. I blocked as much of their view as I could, but Bobby's eyes widened as he stared over my shoulder. There was a faint bruise yellowing on his cheekbone, put there by his father, a bruise that had brought us all here to this moment.

Amanda had started to cry. Tears slid from the corners of her eyes, but she made no sound. A survival tactic. Weep without noise, don't attract unwanted attention, and you wouldn't get "cuffed," as Anita had put it.

From inside my briefcase I brought out a cheap stuffed pony. It was small and bedazzled, and its mane looked like it had been glued on instead of sewn. I held it out to Amanda. "I heard you liked horses," I said. She reached out without looking at the toy and took it from me, holding it at her side in loose fingers.

Bobby had stopped watching his mother and was studying me, sizing me up. His own survival tactic. Could he sit here and resist, or did I mean business? It took a dozen seconds or so of us looking at one another before he finally nodded.

"Come on, Manda. Let's go," Bobby said, his voice flat and resigned. We went.

It was still raining outside, and I'd forgotten my umbrella. I hurried the kids through the downpour to the back seat of my car as the deputy wrestled their mother out of the house behind us. Her hands were cuffed behind her back, but she was still fighting, still calling out to leave her kids alone, and I couldn't help wondering where this Anita had been all the times her husband had lain hands on their children. As quickly as the cynical thought came, it was banished by reality.

That wasn't how this worked.

In the family unit things like morality and justice and right didn't always hold sway. Sometimes a tarnished sense of love reversed things in a weird mirror image of what should be. Normal became split lips and bruises and inappropriate touching. The rotten center of a fine-looking fruit.

I knew this better than anyone.

As the deputy hauled Anita toward the back of his car in a strange simulacrum of her children, I saw she'd gotten a claw in his cheek and raked a bloody path there. I stood back to give them enough room, and when they passed she spit in my face, her saliva hot and thick among the cool rain coating my skin.

"Fucking bastards," she said, her eyes daggers stabbing both of us. "Hope you can sleep at night, you fuckers."

I wiped the spit away and stood in the rain until the deputy had reversed and pulled away. Then I slid into the driver's seat and sat for a second, finally looking up to meet the two sets of eyes staring back in the rearview mirror.

———

Rose Palaver had done better than me and remembered her umbrella.

She stood in a long red rain slicker at the curb in front of a house she shared with her husband and between one and five wards of the state at any given time. The Palavers had been registered temporary-care providers for more than a dozen years. They were both in their late sixties but youthful in their nearly constant motion and positivity. *I'm like a top*, Rose had told me once after I dropped off toddler triplets who had been left unattended for two days in their apartment. *If I quit moving, I'll fall over.*

Now she smiled through the rain as I pulled to a stop and turned to the back seat. "You're going to be staying with Mrs. and Mr. Palaver for a couple of days until your mom can come get you, okay?" No answer from either of the kids. They'd shut down for the most part, just enduring until the next inevitable change in their lives came. I pictured driftwood, gray and listless, at the mercy of the sea until it washed ashore out of the reach of uncaring tides, and had to bite the inside of my lip.

Rose huddled over the kids as soon as they got out of the car, shielding them from the rain. "Hello to you both," she said, her voice warm and sure over the sound of the storm. "I'm Rose. Let's get you inside. Mr. Palaver has some hot cocoa waiting." Our eyes met, and I nodded a thank you. She was up to speed on the kids' situation, knew it could be two days or a year before they were moved to another foster home or back in with their parents. I watched them walk away, Bobby actually taking Rose's hand when she held it out to him. They didn't look back at me, and I couldn't blame them. I was the bad guy, the boogeyman, someone to be forgotten if they could. I'd taken them from their home and brought them somewhere strange and new. Rose was the kind grandmother who would give them something sweet. This was the deal; we all knew our parts.

Halfway up the walk Amanda's fingers loosened, and she dropped the pony I'd given her. She didn't stop or look down. Rose brought them inside the house with the glowing windows, where it was dry and warm and safe. The door shut and I was alone.

I went up the walk and plucked the cheap toy from a gathering puddle. It was cold and heavy. I could relate.

It was time to go home.

3

Home.

Quiet. Safety. Comfort. Those are the words to describe where I live. It's what a home should be. A respite. A sanctuary. A place where the world outside can't touch you. I made it this way, as different as could be from the place I grew up in.

My home was ten minutes outside Easton, a midsize city two hours southwest of Salem. I lived in a neighborhood called Hillside Acres. It wasn't gated or in any way exclusive, but it lived up to its name, notched into the shoulder of a mountain with great views of the ocean. The lots were spacious and sectioned off by thick swaths of trees. My house sat on a curve, tucked mostly out of sight and hidden from the nearest neighbors, who were close enough to hear but not see.

I pulled into the carport out of the rain and sat for a minute with the engine off, decompressing—a diver rising slow, trying not to get the bends. The rain kept falling, and I hurried through it to the house and inside. Just stepping through the door was enough to do it. The nasty acid knot in my stomach started to unlace. A second later a metallic jingle and the clicking of claws on tile did the rest.

"Merrill, hey, boy, how're you?" I knelt, and my dog barreled into me, turning in circles and licking my hands as if I hadn't seen him six hours ago. Merrill was a sleek, dark-haired mutt, a rescue, not only because I got him from a shelter but because he saved me on a daily basis.

"Hungry? Yeah, course you are. Always hungry."

We made our way through the house. The kitchen, dining room, and living area were all one space, open and flowing. I liked the roominess of the house even though it was more space than a single person needed. That was what the realtor said when I bought it five years before, *More space than you need.* How does anyone know how much space someone else needs?

I poured a cup of chow for Merrill and a glass of wine for me, not bothering to check the time. Long ago I'd stopped letting the hands on the clock tell my own when they could or couldn't pick up a drink.

After changing into dry clothes, I stood at the tall western windows, my reflection meeting me, faint but there. Like the events of the afternoon. Already beginning to fade into yet another difficult and necessary day. This career, this job. This life. I'd chosen it, and it had chosen me. That driftwood I'd associated earlier with the kids had been so much deflection. I was the one at the will of something greater, some deeper tide running through the world and through me.

We all think we have choices, and we do, but we're flotsam too. At the whim of circumstance, the things inside us, something as irritating as chance.

I drank my wine.

As Merrill circled his bed and finally flopped down with a contented grunt to doze off his meal, my phone pinged. A text from my friend Sara Wilson in the child placement division. **Sydney is officially adopted! Cheers!** Below the text was a picture of a man with dark-rimmed glasses beside a woman with frizzy blonde hair. Between them stood a girl of ten, all freckles and barrettes and a smile.

Sydney, who I'd removed from a home where people spoke in closed fists and cigarette burns in inconspicuous places. Sydney—who hadn't said a word for the first five days of being free, who only cried—was smiling now.

I took a long swallow of wine to wash away the lump in my throat and went downstairs.

Some people have dream boards made of cork and aspirations, all the things and places they've fantasized about push-pinned in the hopes of realization. I had something else.

The printer on my workstation desk whirred and clacked, expelling a decent color photo of Sydney and her new family, who would hopefully continue to rebuild her trust of the world. I held it for a second before pinning it to the board in the corner beside my desk. There were perhaps two dozen other photos a lot like Sydney's there. Little boys and girls standing with a new parent or parents, some of the light that had been nearly snuffed out now reentering their eyes. I settled into the office chair and looked at the collection of faces.

Very few people had seen the board, and I guarded it with a deep sense of pride tinged with embarrassment. It seemed corny in a superficial way, to put up their pictures and keep them as a shrine of success stories—a reminder for why I kept doing what I did. But I didn't care. Seeing them made me happy, and if I couldn't find joy in helping them, then what the hell was I even doing?

At the bottom of the corkboard, a small silver pendant hung by its chain. The pendant depicted a canonized man carrying a child, and seeing it, the first thought would be Saint Christopher, the patron saint of travelers. But this was Saint Anthony, Anthony of Padua, carer of the weak and sick, patron saint of lost things. It had been my brother Paul's, the last thing he'd given me besides my life.

My wine was gone.

Halfway up the stairs to refill the glass, my phone rang. Byron's name and photo filled up the screen. Byron with his nice, even teeth and wry grin that crinkled the skin around his eyes. Sweet Byron, who had a way with his hands and mouth that unlocked my knees some-times. I almost let the call go to voice mail.

"Hello?"

"Hey, where are you?"

"Home. Why?"

"Guessing you don't have the TV on."

I moved without thinking to the living room, where a flat screen was mounted on the wall, and picked up the remote. "What channel?"

"Doesn't matter."

He was right. The current station happened to be a major news net-work, and a grim-faced grayhair had just finished preparing the viewer for the following disturbing images.

The scene changed to an overhead shot of the ocean, swelling and rolling in the midst of a storm. The same storm peppering the windows with rain, I realized, seeing the chyron on the bottom of the screen: **Volk family feared dead after plane crash**. A handful of rescue boats circled a sprawl of detritus, a few legible numbers and letters surfacing for a moment on a plane's tail section. The shot changed to another angle and showed the crew of a boat hauling a blurred limp form over the side that could only be a body.

The strength in my legs seeped away, and I sat on the couch. Would've sat on the floor if it hadn't been there. I tried setting my wineglass down on the nearest surface, but it slipped off and bounced on the carpet without breaking.

"You see it?" Byron asked in my ear, and I flinched, forgetting he was still on the line.

"Yeah," I said. "Holy shit. Who was on board?"

"All of them."

Something in my chest squeezed painfully, and I saw Mason Roberts sitting across from me, quiet, not meeting my eyes while I studied the marks on his neck that looked like hands.

"Are there—" I had to clear my throat. "Did anyone survive?"

15

"Kaylee was airlifted. She was banged up pretty bad from what I hear, but they think she's going to make it."

"What the hell happened?"

"No one knows for sure, but"—I pictured Byron looking around, checking to see if any other law enforcement were in earshot—"the witness who called the crash in said he thought the pilot and copilot were struggling."

"What?"

"Yeah," Byron said. "And that's where this gets fucking weird." I muted the TV, cutting off the news anchor's solemn but steady voice midsentence. "A coast guard officer told me there were no reported Maydays from the plane before it went down."

For a second Kaylee Volk's Barbie-perfect face and blonde hair floated in my mind's eye, her perky head tilt and smile at the end of every influencer video she'd ever posted. "So what are you saying?"

Byron paused, his voice growing even lower. "They're thinking the crash wasn't an accident."

4

School shopping can be fun! Getting kids geared up for school | Kaylee Volk

70,134 views * Aug 15, 2022

Kaylee Volk (Volks At Home)

723k subscribers

SCHOOL SHOPPING TIPS Some ideas and tips for managing what can be a very stressful time of year. Anyone with kids knows how challenging clothes and supplies shopping can be, but I'm sharing some ways to make a chore into a family-fun excursion! Follow along as I take our three foster children, Andrea, Mason, and Bethany, to four major retailers to get the sup . . .

SHOW MORE

Video Plays

Upbeat intro music and a graphic of two adult figures holding hands with three kids appears on the screen, then fades away.

Kaylee Volk's face fills up the screen, and she smiles.

KAYLEE
(overly perky)
Hi, everyone! Thanks so much for tuning in. We have a great episode today, which involves one of my most favorite things in the world. You guessed it—shopping! I'm taking the kids school shopping and will be giving you all some tips on how to turn what can be a chore into a fun-filled family expedition!

The scene cuts to a kitchen table with three kids sitting around it. Andrea Parish (18) sits closest, purposely ignoring the camera. Mason Roberts (14) sits across from her, looking down into his bowl of cereal. Bethany Jacobs (9) grins and hams it up while holding a large purple teddy bear.

KAYLEE (O.S.)
Okay, guys, are we ready for a fun day at the mall?

BETHANY
Yeah!

ANDREA
(sarcastic)
Yeah!

KAYLEE (O.S.)
Mason?

Mason finally glances up and smiles halfheartedly. He gives her a shy thumbs-up.

Kaylee turns the camera on herself.

KAYLEE

Don't worry about these party poopers. I guess I'll be proving to them as well as you at home that shopping can be a good time.

BETHANY

Let's go! Let's go!

Justin Volk (28) enters the kitchen. He's got a towel around his neck, and sweat stains the front of his T-shirt.

KAYLEE

And there's the man of the house. How was your workout, babe?

JUSTIN

A real butt kicker. That's why I'm refueling with Amino Blast Recovery.

Justin holds up a sports drink container, which Kaylee pans away from.

KAYLEE (O.S.)

(teasing)

Get your shameless product plug out of my video and on your own channel!

Justin laughs.

Scene transitions to Kaylee sitting in the driver's seat of a van. She blinks before smiling beatifically. She starts to talk, then swallows thickly. It's apparent she's biting back tears.

KAYLEE

So I just wanted to take a moment with you guys before the kids climb in.

(beat)

I want to say to all of you parents out there struggling right now, whether it be with your kid's behavior or making ends meet or whatever it is, it's okay to be sad sometimes. It's okay to be angry. It's okay to be hurt by their actions or words. As parents we're supposed to be superheroes and never let anything get to us, but that's not true. We're people just like anyone, and we need care too.

(beat)

So it's okay to care for yourself and take a break when you need one. In fact I'll share with you what I do—I recently started using this great new brand of bubble bath called SpaDream.

Kaylee holds up a tiny bottle of the bubble bath and smiles.

HIGH SPEED SCRUBBING

Video Plays

On the screen Bethany bounces along beside Kaylee, who's pushing a cart through a large department store. Kaylee seems to be wearing a type of GoPro camera, which records whatever she looks at.

BETHANY

(singsong)

I love shop-ping, I love shop-ping. Shop, shop, shop-ping.

KAYLEE (O.S.)

Not so loud, Bethy.

There's a swift shot of Bethany's hurt expression before the camera pans away.

KAYLEE (O.S.)

Okay, now where did Mason get to? Oh, there he is. You finding everything okay, Mase?

Mason is picking out boxer shorts. He glances at the camera, eyes widening in mortification before turning away. Kaylee laughs. Bethany mimics her.

KAYLEE (O.S.)

And now where is Andrea? She was supposed to be looking at shoes, but I don't see her . . .

BETHANY

There she is!

Bethany points, and the camera follows her finger. Andrea stands in a center aisle of lingerie holding a silk teddy.

KAYLEE (O.S.)

Andrea! What are you doing?

Andrea flinches but then takes her time putting the lingerie back. She gives Kaylee, then the camera, a withering look before walking past.

ANDREA

(flat)

Looking at shoes.

A beat where Kaylee seems at a loss, the camera moving back to Bethany, who raises her eyebrows and blinks.

The scene cuts to a close-up of Kaylee, who appears stoic. The background suggests she is back home.

KAYLEE

Okay, so I wanted to close out the video by addressing some of your prior comments about Andrea. You've noticed the same as Justin and I have that she's become more moody in the last few months. I want to remind everyone watching that she came from a pretty terrible situation, and until she was placed with us, she never had a stable environment. That's all we've ever dreamed of is to give these kids a loving and supportive home.

A pause, and again Kaylee appears on the verge of tears. She swipes once at her eyes.

Sorry, it's just been a little hard. But we're doing really good! Andrea's excited to be going to college next fall, and she'll be staying in state, so we'll still be able to see her a lot, and hopefully she'll continue to appear on the channel. I'm thinking actually the next video is going to be about transitions. We'll sit down with Andrea and go over everything she's apprehensive about. It'll be a great learning experience for those of you at home with teenagers transitioning to college. And I know you all have been asking about when the next flight video will be—it's coming soon! We're planning a trip up the coast in a few weeks and should have some amazing content for you. Until next time, stay safe, healthy, and happy, from all of us here at the Volk house. Bye!

Video Ends

5

The child services department is located in a single-story county building on the northern side of town, hidden behind a strip mall. It's the
color of sand, the color of forgetting. I think they made it that way
on purpose because who wants to remember the people who have no
choice but to go there and fill out forms so they can get money to pay
rent or vouchers to buy groceries? Who wants to look at those people
with anything other than disdain and self-righteousness?

It was after hours when I arrived, only a few cars in the parking
lot—one of them particularly annoying in its presence. I'd hoped Kelly
would have gone home by now, but he was still here, burning the 6:00
p.m. oil.

Hurrying past my boss's glassed-in office didn't work as well as I'd
hoped. I was almost to my cubicle where I could duck down out of
sight and do what I'd come here for when Jim Kelly's dry voice floated
down the hall after me.

"Nora, what are you doing here?"

I half turned and kept moving. You had to keep moving when it
came to Kelly, otherwise he'd drain your will like some kind of energy
vampire. "Checking something."

"How'd the removal go this afternoon?"

"As good as any of them do." Then I was at my cubicle's entrance
and out of sight and hopefully out of Kelly's mind. I didn't want him

ambling down to chitchat about what I was doing here for two reasons. One, my supervisor bothered me on some soulless managerial level, and two—I didn't know.

I sat at my desk for a full minute, not moving, trying to figure it out. Shock had come and gone on the drive into work. Any type of disbelief associated with this job has a seriously short half-life. It has to be that way or otherwise you'd always be like a bombing survivor, wandering through the rubble of someone else's life. You form calluses that look suspiciously like scars and you keep doing your job because there's always another family, another kid who's suffering through a special kind of hell, and you have to do what you can.

I did what I could.

———

I started with the Volk case file pulled up on my desktop. It wasn't even two months old, still fresh in the system's history and in my own. The Volks were one of the youngest foster couples in the state. They possessed a semifamous last name, at least in a short radius around the city center, since Justin's father had started Volk Investments thirty years ago and built it into one of the premier private money management firms on the West Coast. Justin worked at his father's firm as a junior manager, but everyone knew (including him) that he'd be taking the reins someday from the old man.

Kaylee Volk was a little more of a mystery. She was pretty in that strange airbrushed way that didn't look real. Like if you walked up to her she'd become a smiling cardboard cutout holding some kind of sponsored product on display. I didn't know much about her other than she'd come from a foster home herself and that she'd built a significant online following as an influencer. As far as influencers go, content is king. And in this particular case, Kaylee's content was her family.

The Volks had started things off a few years prior by fostering, then adopting Bethany Jacobs, who was only seven at the time. When I'd interviewed them after the incident involving their other two children, Mason and Andrea, Kaylee had said they couldn't have kids of their own. She'd stated this with a smile that was painful to look at. Originally Bethany had been put in foster care for neglect—her parents having gotten in the habit of going on meth-fueled binges where they would disappear for days, leaving Bethany alone to fend for herself. Which she did quite well until a neighbor reported the little girl next door was up at all hours watching Japanese anime so loudly it woke her in the middle of the night.

Next came Mason Roberts—a quiet boy of thirteen when the Volks took him in. Mason had been abused in almost every way imaginable by a mother diagnosed later with Munchausen by proxy. Mason had failed to thrive due to malnourishment. He walked with a limp because of a broken femur that had never been set and healed badly. He was bookish and quiet and reserved to the point his teachers stated they sometimes forgot he was in their classes. It seemed he was also a little too quiet for the Volks. I had my suspicions that Kaylee wanted some turmoil between older brother and younger sister along with the cute sibling "aww" moments that warmed the hearts of subscribers. As a species we like spectacle along with the nice stories. We get off on it. As long as it's not *our* issue, *our* problem, *our* pain. When it's removed from us, it's something else. It's entertainment.

Enter Andrea Parish.

Seventeen when she became an honorary Volk, as Kaylee sometimes put it in her videos. Pretty and blonde with black roots showing, too much eye shadow, a trace of punk about her that was almost like a warning. Touch me and lose a finger. Or a hand. And she could back it up. Andrea had been in no less than four foster homes since being removed from her biological father's care after he put her in the hospital with a fractured orbital bone and a broken jaw to match. A colleague of mine had been the one to place Andrea in her first foster home, and he said later there was something about the girl that had left him a little off-center. She'd had a frightening determination about her almost like an aura, something tangible that said, *I am not a victim, and you better not treat me that way, or I'll prove you wrong. I'll make you sorry.*

In the weeks and months after her first placements, Andrea made good on that initial impression.

She quarreled with the other two foster kids and had to be moved to a home without any other children from which she promptly stole $400 in cash and ran away. Ditto for the next two placements. Steal, run away, buy drugs, break and enter, fight, drink, run some more. For Andrea it was a never-ending cycle of trouble and resetting. It was like if she could just steal enough or run far enough, she'd distance herself from what had happened to her. From what was inside her.

Over time Andrea became somewhat of a pariah in the county system, a trouble child among troubled children, and there'd been talk of shipping her south to a larger group facility—the equivalent of shoving a broken lamp out of sight into the back of the closet, the one you know you can't fix but can't bear to throw away.

Then the Volks reached out, asking if there was an older child they could take in, someone closer to adulthood than single digits who would round out their family. It was like providence, though there were rumbles in the office and bets being made behind backs about how long Andrea would last in the influencer household. But she surprised everyone by going quiet, by staying put, by getting along with her foster siblings. Until last month.

———

Teachers are something called mandated reporters. If they see a kid coming in with bruises and cuts that aren't natural, they are legally obligated to alert the authorities. Authorities like me.

26

So when I got a call on a Tuesday morning back in early September to come to Gordon High, it wasn't unusual. Child services receives more calls from teachers about abuse or neglect than you'd think. More than you'd want to believe.

Mason Roberts was in a counselor's office, sitting in a chair in the corner, reading a book. *Fahrenheit 451* I saw as I came in and sat down across from him. And something in me clicked.

Paul had loved to read. Had taught me and my younger brother, Stephen, how. He'd loved Bradbury even at twelve. Maybe because he was twelve.

So when I saw that book in Mason's hands, there was a collision of time and space, and for a second I was nine again, locked away in the dark—hunger boring a hole in my stomach like a parasite, and Paul's voice retelling *Something Wicked This Way Comes* to us in his own words.

Mason's neck was a collage of discolored skin, like someone had taken a palette of blues and blacks and used the flesh above his collarbones to finger paint on. I introduced myself and made the regular small talk to get him comfortable, but it didn't work with Mason. He was too smart to be put off by my questions about his book or his classes. He knew why I was there.

Andrea had done it, he said. They'd had a fight, and it had gotten out of control. But they were okay now. Had made up. *When did this happen?* I asked. *Two nights ago* was his reply, quiet, without looking at me. *What was the fight about?* A shrug. Something stupid; he couldn't remember.

Some child services workers are investigators. Literally. They ask questions, search out clues, sift through statements just like a detective. You have to know how to interview and ask the right things. You have to know how to smell a lie amid the truth.

Mason was lying.

But no matter how I maneuvered or rearranged the questioning, his answers stayed the same. Simple and to the point. He was a locked door. But compared to him, Andrea was a vault.

She slouched in the same chair Mason had sat in before I sent him back to class. She wore a short skirt toeing the line of school regs and a crop top emblazoned with the words Bog Ape—a band, she told me, one I'd never heard of. Her eye shadow was darker than the picture in her file, and she stared at me out of it with an open challenge. *I've seen your kind before. Try me, lady. This is nothing new.*

I took in the scar on her cheek where her father's fist had split her wide open when she was only fifteen. Noted the light scratches on her arm and wondered if they'd come from Mason's nails. She was every kid who had ever been treated terribly. She was singular. She was me.

Andrea wouldn't admit to choking Mason, would only say everything was fine now. *Ask him, everything's okay.* I told her the consequences weren't up to Mason. They were up to me. I asked if she liked living with the Volks, if the environment was safe and a good fit. Her posture changed. She sat straighter, smoothed her skirt. A nod. That was all she'd give me. *Do you like it there?* Another nod. I asked when her birthday was. She told me a little over a month ago. *Are the Volks planning on letting you stay with them for the rest of the school year? Yes,* she said, and her eyes finally lost their shine of defiance and dropped to her lap. She knew the stakes as well as I did. The Volks were well off, lived in a big house in a nice neighborhood. Could help her with college or boot her at any time since she was an adult.

When I realized I wasn't going to get the story behind the fight, I told her the deal. Assaulting your younger foster sibling was a wholly different animal than stealing some cash and running off into the night. I'd be interviewing her foster parents, then drawing up a care plan. The plan would dictate conditions and requirements she would have to abide by for as long as she resided with the Volks. If those conditions were met, everything would go on as normal. If they weren't . . .

I didn't have to spell it out. She knew this was her last chance.

Andrea left the counselor's office, giving the officer who'd accompanied me a cursory glance, then was gone into the labyrinth of the school's hallways and stairs. That was the last time I saw her before the plane crash.

———

Now I sat motionless before the screen in my cubicle, mind whirring like the fan inside the computer. I don't know what I'd expected to find in the file I hadn't already gone over in my head. All the parameters of the care plan had been met. The Volks had appeared in court with Andrea; likewise, Andrea had completed the mandated therapy sessions So had Mason. The case had grown quiet like it was supposed to when the system was actually working.

And yet something had felt off. Wrong.

There was nothing for me to put my finger on, nothing that jumped out and screamed a warning to intervene, but somewhere deep inside me, an ill-tuned piano was playing a sour note over and over. Had been ever since meeting Andrea and Mason. Both kids had been holding back, that was clear to anyone who took five minutes to read the file. But why? If it was just a teenaged disagreement that had gotten out of hand, why play dumb about it?

The overhead lights snapped off, and the cubicles fell into darkness— Kelly leaving for the night. I waited in the partitioned gloom for something to come to me. Some revelation other than the festering unease and the growing sense of guilt.

You could have done something. The internal voice got me up and out of the chair, but it didn't stay in the cubicle. It followed like some personal storm cloud, hovering and raining doubt.

You knew something was off, but you couldn't be bothered, were too busy to dig in and root out the problem.

I made it to my car. The rain had tapered off while I was inside, but the wind was up, and it bullied me, tugged at my hair, shoved the car door closed almost before I could get my leg inside.

This is on you. You missed something.

"Stop," I said aloud. And for once the doubt inside me fell quiet. But it was a gloating silence. Because I knew it wasn't just aftershocks of shock or recalling how Mason reminded me of my dead brother. The voice was right.

I'd made a mistake somewhere.

6

Byron was sitting on my front porch when I got home.

He was still in uniform, shirt open at the throat, his duty belt probably locked away in his car. A bag of Chinese takeout sat on the stoop beside him, and he held a bottle of wine loosely in one hand. He looked exhausted but gave me a smile equal parts knowing and sad, and the excuse I was going to give him about not wanting company thinned and broke apart.

Okay. Okay.

———

The food was good, and the conversation was better because there wasn't any. Byron didn't have the best judgment about when to leave me alone, but he knew when to be quiet. Basically a wash.

The wine was going down easy, and I'd already refilled my glass twice. The wind nudged at the house, which creaked reassuringly, letting me know it was doing its job keeping out the weather. Merrill snoozed at my feet, issuing a snore every so often.

When we were done eating we cleaned up, and Byron took it upon himself to wash the few dishes we'd dirtied. I didn't like how he knew where I kept the soap or the scrub pads, how comfortable he was getting with my place, but filed the irritation away to be examined later. Or never.

"Doing okay?" he said after draining the dishwater and joining me by the tall windows. I'd refilled my glass from a second bottle of wine and took a long swallow before answering.

"No. Not really."

"Spoke to one of the EMTs who life-flighted Kaylee. He said it was touch and go, but if he had to guess, she was going to pull through."

"Did they recover everyone—all the other bodies?"

Byron paused. "Just the boy's so far."

"Mason. His name was Mason." I blew out a long breath and took another drink, unconsciously-consciously moving a step away from him. Christ, it wasn't Byron's fault he didn't know their names by heart. That was my job. But even so I was the odd one at work, always making it a point to know the kids' stories, where they came from and where they were going, keeping track of them best I could. We were all overburdened with cases. Kids, kids, and more kids needing help, coming out of the woodwork as if there was no end to them because there wasn't. Child welfare—underfunded, understaffed, underappreciated, just like any other state service that actually was set up to do some good—and all the while the public wondering why things were so bad in the juvenile community. Wondering where exactly their tax dollars were going.

I wanted to scream into every haughty face, break every wagging finger, muzzle every chiding, privileged voice. Instead I took it out on my boyfriend.

"Sorry," I said quietly. "Trying to make sense of it."

Byron set his wine down and came up behind me, put his hands on my shoulders and squeezed. His hands were strong, and the pressure was delicious. "I don't think I ever told you about my very first day on the job," he said, kneading the muscles in my neck, which were beginning to loosen. "I got assigned to patrol on a stretch of highway north on forty-six. It's quiet, no speeders, which is what I was sent up there for to break me in. So I pull into a little roadside café, and there's this boy playing soccer near the parking lot. He's kicking the ball, and it's rolling close to the highway. I talk to him. Tell him he should move closer to the restaurant so his ball doesn't go out into the street. His parents come over, we have a quick chat, they thank me, the boy waves, and I wave back. I remember that really clearly, how he waved with his whole arm, really put some energy into it."

Byron paused and his hands stilled as well. "Twenty minutes later I get a call to respond to a crash five miles from the café. It's the family I just talked to. They got T-boned by a drunk running a red light. And the whole time I'm trying to pry them out of this crushed tin can their car is, looking for vitals that aren't there, I'm thinking they had to pass through that intersection at the perfect time, and I was part of that timing. I talked to their son to keep him out of harm's way and helped get them all killed because of it."

I stared at Byron's reflection in the glass, his face barely there over my shoulder.

"We do what we do to help. That's all. You look further than that and you'll drive yourself insane."

I wanted to protest, to say this was different because he hadn't known, hadn't had any warning about what was to come, and I did. On some instinctual level I'd felt something was wrong at the Volk household but hadn't gone the extra mile. I kept this inside because I already knew what Byron's response would be. He'd say I'd done what I was supposed to, no one was going to blame me for what happened. And he wasn't wrong—I wasn't legally culpable in that family's demise. But legality didn't enter into the inner sanctum where things held true sway. Those 2:00 a.m. thoughts and the sharp edges of guilt weren't admissible in court, but they were a prison all their own. He wouldn't want to hear it, but we are all responsible in one way or another.

We're all to blame.

Byron released my shoulders and slipped his arms around my waist, pressed himself up against me. He smelled of faint cologne, wine, and the day's sweat. His lips found the junction of my shoulder and neck, and my stomach did a familiar plunge, like I'd stepped off an unexpected ledge. When I'd gotten home, intimacy was the very last thing on my mind. But now, with his lips and hint of stubble moving up my neck to the spot behind my ear, a switch flipped inside me.

What followed was an acceleration of need. Clothes coming off gradually, then ripped away. The kind of passion where you barely make it to the bed. It escalated into aggressive territory for me—suddenly knowing exactly what I needed and taking it as firmly and quickly as I could. A frantic release that pulsed and sprawled for minutes before fading into a comforting silence punctuated only by the wind.

———

I woke hours later. The wind had cleared the clouds away, and the moon cut cool bars of light across the bedroom floor. Byron slept solidly beside me, one arm thrown over my waist. I'd always marveled at how soundly others slumbered. Their minds could shut down and leave them be for hours at a time, while mine always seemed to be in third gear, just waiting to drop the clutch and burn rubber the moment I surfaced.

My phone told me it was three fifteen. The clock in my head said that was all the sleep I was going to get. I rose without waking Byron, both appreciative and annoyed at the sight of him in my bed. We'd have to talk about this at some point, but that could wait.

My robe, a cup of tea from the kitchen, then the overstuffed chair in the living room looking out the windows onto the deck. This was the place I came to when sleep washed me ashore and stranded me awake. It was the most open of all the rooms in the house, with the broadest windows. I never labeled myself as claustrophobic, but I was.

It was apparent in all the wide spaces of the house, the doors removed from all the bedroom closets so they became walk-ins. Full darkness usually bothered me, too, but tonight I didn't even need to turn on a floor lamp with the moon hanging where it was. Tonight I could see everything—even the things I didn't want to.

Paul sat in the chair in the corner where it was the darkest. He was twelve, forever twelve, and so skinny he barely made a dent in the cushions. Paul, beautiful, quiet Paul, who loved Stephen and me so much—more than we knew until it was too late. Paul sighed, and it sounded like the wind.

———

Our father had control issues. That was how our mother put it before she disappeared. It wasn't the first time she'd vanished from our day-to-day existence—we'd come to half expect the morning when she wouldn't be at the breakfast table, a cigarette between her pointer and middle fingers of her right hand, bushy hair barely tied back from a steaming coffee cup. She was an artist, a free spirit who painted in abstracts and spoke in them too. *When you dream, the truth appears,* she'd tell us. *You just have to sift it free from all the other pieces.* For our family the truth was she and our father couldn't have been more different.

How our parents met is lost knowledge—an archeological dig neither I nor Stephen wanted to exhume. Both of them were only children without any other close relatives. Transplants to the coast from the Midwest. Our father was a decade older than our mother, yet another indication they might've believed opposites attracted or the gap in their spectrum would balance out.

Think of a man who appreciates numbers. You can already see him in your head—bookish, tall, glasses, hair parted on the side, serious, quiet. He's meticulous and always on time. You know someone like him. He's an accountant who prefers spreadsheets and quarterly reports to words. If he needs to communicate at work, it's through brief emails. At home he uses notes like **DO NOT LEAVE TOOTHPASTE IN THE SINK** taped to the bathroom mirror or **SWEEP FLOOR** attached to the fridge with a magnet.

Other times he uses the back of his hand to lash across your face. That was our father.

If he decided to speak with his hands, you'd suddenly be on the floor at his feet, fighting a traitorous bladder from releasing while he towered over you. *The garbage smells,* he would say in a thin voice like a reed catching a gust of wind. Our mother would be conspicuously absent during these episodes, her attention desperately needed elsewhere in the house until the violence had passed. Looking back I'm sure she received her own form of punishment, which was most likely why she left and never returned. On the good days our father would come home after work, take his briefcase into his office, and sometimes we wouldn't see him for the rest of the night. Though once in a while I woke to the sound of him moving around in the house after we'd gone to bed. I wondered what he was doing but never got up the courage to go see.

In my nightmares a thing with dragging feet would come slowly down the hall and stop in front of my room, the pause a specific kind of torture before my door opened and a tall shape slumped through. It would stand over my bed with whistling breath and two white discs of thick glasses where the eyes should've been, and I would wait, wait for it to touch me, to hurt me, to kill me, but it never did. I'd wake to a lingering smell of my father's aftershave in the air and wonder if I'd been dreaming at all.

When our mother finally flew the coop indefinitely, Paul took over her duties. He cooked, cleaned, made sure Stephen and I had lunch money in our accounts. He maneuvered us out of our father's way as much as possible, but even so there were . . . incidents.

Like the time Stephen forgot his foam bat and ball set on the front lawn, and our father brought it inside and made Stephen hold the ball in his mouth for the better part of six hours as tears streamed in silent tracks down his small face. Or when he caught me trying on some of our mother's clothes she'd left behind in their bedroom. I hadn't heard him come home, only found myself suddenly sprawled in the corner, the back of my head on fire from where he slammed his briefcase into it. He'd shown me the rifle then for the first time. Taken it out from under the side of the bed our mother no longer slept on and pressed its muzzle up against my eye. He told me to look inside it and tell him what I saw. Shaking and sobbing, I said, *Darkness*. It seemed to appease him.

I could still feel the cold ring of steel there when I thought about it.

But Paul kept us as safe as he could, maybe even then sensing the catastrophic danger, like an animal will know an earthquake or tsunami is going to hit before the sirens go off.

When the inevitable happened, it was my fault.

The bathroom sink leaked. A steady stream unless you turned the handle just right. One morning, around six months after our mother left, we were in a hurry leaving for school, and I'd washed my face in the stoppered sink but hadn't pulled the plug. We came home that afternoon to water having invaded the hall, the kitchen, our father's bedroom, the entry. It was running down the walls in the basement and pooling on the floor beneath the washer and dryer.

We tried to clean it up. We tried.

Paul hid us in his bedroom closet when our father came home. Stephen and I crouched there, listening, waiting for something, some outburst from the silent monster we tiptoed around, but none came. The quiet was worse—a steel wire being drawn tighter and tighter until it hummed with tension. It finally snapped with the closet door coming open and Paul being thrown inside. The sound of a cordless drill came a few minutes later, screws boring into wood, then footsteps slowly receding to nothing. When we tried the door, it wouldn't move, wouldn't budge an inch. We sat in the dark, holding one another.

Waiting.

———

My tea was cold, and the moonlight had shifted into the corner. Paul wasn't in the chair anymore. I was alone again.

7

Forensic interview transcript, case file: 12090-Volk.
Date: 9/6/2022
State representative: Nora McTavish, CPS
Witness: Justin Volk

NM: *This is Nora McTavish with state child services conducting an inter-view with foster parent Justin Volk concerning an incident between Andrea Parish and Mason Roberts, who reside in his home under the care of he and his wife, Kaylee. Good morning, Justin.*
JV: *Morning.*
NM: *So I wanted to start by just laying out a few basic points for the record. Could you state your age?*
JV: *I'm twenty-eight.*
NM: *And where do you work?*
JV: *At Volk Investments. It's my father's business.*
NM: *And how long have you and your wife been foster parents?*
JV: *Uh ... I think it's almost three years now. Bethany came to live with us in December of 2019.*
NM: *And why did you decide to become foster parents?*
JV: *We weren't able to have kids of our own, so, yeah ...*
NM: *Okay. So the incident we're discussing today occurred three days ago on the night of the third. Can you tell me what happened?*
JV: *See that's the thing, and I told the school superintendent this—we didn't know anything was wrong until they called. I didn't hear the fight, and neither of the kids said anything the next morning.*

NM: *You said "I." Where was your wife?*
JV: *Out of town for a conference.*
NM: *And you didn't see the bruising on Mason's neck? It was noticeable.*
JV: (Pause) *No, I don't remember seeing it, but we were in a hurry that morning.*
NM: *Why?*
JV: *Excuse me?*
NM: *Why were you in a hurry?*
JV: *I don't remember. I think we all woke up late.*
NM: *And you brought the kids to school, correct? Not Kaylee?*
JV: *Right.*
NM: *And how did they seem?*
JV: *Fine. Totally fine. Their usual selves.*
NM: *Nothing seemed off to you? No unusual tension between Andrea and Mason?*
JV: *No, not that sticks out. But I could've missed it. Like I said, we were running late.*
NM: *So prior to the incident, do you recall any disagreements between the two of them?*
JV: *No.*
NM: *Any changes going on in the household that could be upsetting?*
JV: *No. Everything's fine.*
NM: *How about your wife's career? She's what you'd call an influencer, right?*
JV: *I mean, yes. She's a vlogger who features our family and lifestyle on her channel.*
NM: *And do you think that could be putting any type of pressure on the children?*
JV: *No. We always talk to the kids before doing an update. Make sure they're comfortable with whatever Kaylee's got planned.*
NM: *And they've never had a problem?*
JV: *No. Go ahead and ask them.*
NM: *I have.* (Pause)
JV: *So, I mean, the kids aren't going to be . . . taken away or anything crazy like that, are they?*
NM: *We're still trying to understand what happened and why at this point. The care plan we come up with will determine the next steps.*
JV: *And we means you, right? Or the state?*
NM: *Yes, to an extent.*
JV: *I just want to say that we're not that type of family.*

NM: *What type is that?*
JV: *You know, the problem kind. We're good people. It was just a fight. Kids fight all the time. I know I got into scuffles when I was a teenager, I'm sure you did too. It wouldn't be fair to them that they get taken from the best home they've ever been in just because of a misunderstanding.*
NM: *That's what I'm here to determine. I need to know what caused this to make sure we can address it so it doesn't happen again.* (Pause) *You're sure you don't know what their fight was about?*
JV: *You already asked me that.*
NM: *It's just you said "misunderstanding."*
JV: *I meant—you know how kids can be. They're sensitive, and things can escalate, that's all I'm saying. I just don't want their lives upended because of something like this.*
NM: *Don't worry, Mr. Volk, the care plan will be designed with the very best interest of the children in mind.*
JV: *I hope so. They've been through enough. They don't need anything else to happen to them.*

8

I hadn't even made it to my desk the next morning when Tracy Jenkins, the deputy administrator, handed me a file folder and said there were four fairly urgent emails waiting for me in my inbox.

"What's this?" I asked, the coffee finally making my neurons fire in sequence.

"Jackson's out sick this week. Everyone's taking one of his cases," Tracy said over her shoulder, not slowing down.

Richard Jackson wasn't sick. I was pretty sure of it—unless being allergic to work counted. Since he was a step under Tracy and had seniority over all the rest of us, it wasn't uncommon to find one of his case files on your desk after coming back from the bathroom or lunch with a sticky note on the front, a sugary request to "help him out" punctuated with a hurriedly drawn smiley face. Kelly could've put a stop to the shirking, but the two men apparently had some unsaid agreement, possibly a shared affinity for a particular local bar. Complaints went unaddressed.

In my cubicle, which was a single cog in the greater machine of social services, I sat down and opened the folder. And read. And as I read, something shifted in me. Some other internal gearwork that had been idle engaged and began to turn in anger. It had been less than a year since I'd last felt these particular rpms. Then I was on my feet and moving to Kelly's office.

Days since last pure outrage: zero.

He was just setting his phone down when I walked into his glass cubicle—Kelly's work space transparent and transcendent as leader among the rest of the hive. I dropped the folder on his desk. "What the hell's this?"

"Jackson's off this week. Everyone's—"

"No, I mean this case. Julia Roust."

Kelly sat back in his chair, the very image of administrative zen. An undisturbed pool of humoring. "Enlighten me."

"The police report says her ex-boyfriend forced her out of the house and into his car."

"So she left her child unattended, correct?"

"Under threat of violence."

Kelly sat forward and began to shuffle papers. "Under statute five-five—"

"I know what the statute says. This"—I reached out and tapped the folder—"is bullshit."

"It's not our responsibility to sort through the legal decisions sent over from the courthouse. We carry them out. It's probation with weekly check-ins, not a removal."

"It says in the report she doesn't own a vehicle. How's she supposed to make check-ins without a vehicle?"

"That really isn't our concern."

"It should be."

Kelly rubbed his brow. "I get it. I really do. Fair isn't always a component here, you know that. Honestly Nora, you're the best I have, and it's because of your heart. But your heart gets in the way too. Do you see the DA's signature on that paperwork? See the judge's?" When I didn't answer, he nodded and went back to his paper shuffling. "It's just the job. Go do it."

"You mean do Jackson's job," I said, grabbing the folder from his desk.

"Nora—"

I didn't wait around for whatever platitude he was going to regurgitate, didn't want to hear any more about how "we didn't make the rules" or "the guidelines are there for a reason." The truth was the system was deeply flawed because people were. The law is one size fits all, while reality is a series of chaotic events we raft through like white water. The difference is some people get handed life jackets while others are told they should've learned how to swim better.

Outside, the day was cool, the sky cloudy and migraine bright. I slung the folder into my passenger seat and sat behind the wheel for nearly a minute, attempting to calm down, getting myself aligned to do what needed to be done. I thought of Paul again and wondered if he were disappointed, wondered if he could see me now, would he want to take his sacrifice back.

I punched Julia Roust's address into my phone and started to drive, not really seeing the streets or the other cars—on autopilot while I went somewhere else. It wasn't until I made the final turn and heard my phone explaining we were going the wrong way that I realized where I was.

I coasted into the parking lot and found a spot. Shut the car off.

Okay. Okay.

———

The hospital had the feel of a train station or airport, a bustle and urgency of competing schedules thick in the air. Feet slapped and clacked on the tile floor, and bodies brushed past, all hurrying somewhere else. And then there was me off to the side of the hall without a boarding pass, without a destination.

What was I doing here?

At the nurse's station it took almost five minutes to get someone's attention. I had my ID ready, feeling like there was a line and I was toeing it but couldn't help but show the nurse the hard card and ask which room Kaylee Volk was in. Authority is picture IDs and a commanding tone. That's the world we live in. The nurse barely blinked, just nodded and pointed down the hall. "Room 201. I'm not sure if she'll be awake."

Two steps away from the nurse's station, a guy bumped into me. Our shoulders thudded against one another hard enough to spin me halfway around. I said excuse me to his back as he continued on. No acknowledgment, not even a pause. That's also the world we live in.

Room 201 was private with a short bank of windows facing east. Gray light fell over all manner of medical equipment along with the bed and its occupant. For a beat I thought I had the wrong room. The stick-thin bandaged thing in the bed bore almost no resemblance to the blonde, tan perkiness Kaylee Volk exuded in every video as well as in person. But there beneath a sutured eyebrow and swollen bruises, there among split lips and an arm in a cast was the woman who hundreds of thousands of people looked to for entertainment and advice.

Kaylee's eyes were battered slits, and for a moment the only movement in the room was her heart rate on a green screen and the hourglass-drip of an IV. Then she turned her head and saw me there.

"Ev?" she said weakly.

I cleared my throat and stepped closer. "Hi, Mrs. Volk, I don't know if you remember me. Nora McTavish. I'm with child services." Kaylee stared at me, and even though she didn't say it, I could hear what she was thinking because the same thought was repeating in my head.

What was I doing here?

"I'm sorry to bother you. I can go if you're not feeling up to seeing anyone."

Kaylee gestured with her good arm. "Come in."

I took a seat beside the bed so we were eye level. The two of us, taking a second to absorb each other. I couldn't help but look at her injuries. She gave me a pained half smile.

"Concussion, broken ribs, broken arm, lacerations, bruising. Hypothermia, too, but that's gone now they tell me." There was a muddled softness to her words I associated with heavy drug use.

"I'm very sorry."

"They're . . . they're all . . . they're gone. But I'm still here." Kaylee grimaced, and it was terrible watching her face become a contraction of grief, painful on every level. Without thinking I put a hand lightly on her shoulder. It felt birdlike through the thin fabric of her hospital gown.

"Can you tell me what happened?" I asked. And this was why I was here. No more skirting the truth, no more lying to myself. Like we all do at the end of the day, I wanted to know. "Was there a problem with the plane?"

A tear leaked from the corner of Kaylee's left eye. It looked like fluid weeping from a wound. "I don't know why." She paused, struggling to see through her tears, to study the room as if trying to hold on to consciousness. "I tried . . . tried to stop her."

"Excuse me?" a voice said from behind me.

A nurse stood in the doorway, arms folded, head tilted forward, chin tucked in like a boxer. "I'm sorry, but you shouldn't be in here. Mrs. Volk needs her rest."

I turned back to Kaylee, and her slitted eyes were closing, opening, closing more. Staying closed. I squeezed her shoulder a little, bringing her back for a second. "Who, Kaylee? Tried to stop who?"

"Ma'am?" The nurse's voice was an ice pick.

Kaylee licked her cracked lips, tongue rasping over stitches. "Andrea," she said, and found me with her drug-lacquered gaze one last time before drifting away. "Andrea did it."

9

The name of the woman who took our hands and led us out of the close, dark hell of the closet was Estrella. Her name is Spanish for star, and my brother and I fixed our gazes on her like she was one as she took us out of our childhood home to which we'd never return.

Later I understood why she did it, why she told us to look at her—*Watch me, keep your eyes on me, okay?* Estrella thought if she could keep our attention focused on her, we wouldn't notice the words. Those huge blocky letters scrawled in black paint across the walls. All those words our father hated so much he kept them inside until they curdled and festered and rotted him from the center out. Before he'd taken his rifle up to the roof of the building he worked in, he lanced some of the infection by writing out those secret thoughts. Things like WE AREN'T REAL, and, THEIR LAUGHTER IS LIKE BREATHING SMOKE, and one in particular I think about a lot—NONE OF THIS IS HAPPENING.

None of this is happening.

The words of a madman—a madman who locked his children in a closet and who went on to add himself to an unending list of madmen—and yet those words resonated and came back to me often.

None of this is happening.

I almost said it as I sat in my car outside Julia Roust's home. I'd gone to the hospital because I needed to know about the Volks. About why their plane went down. Because somewhere in the distant past, which is always close by, a faucet was still running. A sink was overflowing. Rooms were flooding—water seeping into carpet and filling cracks in the floor, creeping ever outward.

Andrea did it.

Andrea crashed the plane.

Andrea, the punk, the troubled child, the battered girl who refused to ever be hurt again, so she hurt others. She'd crashed the plane. I'd wanted to put myself at ease by knowing and had stepped on a land mine instead.

I closed my eyes, let my head rest forward on the steering wheel. Traffic sang by off-key. The wind had come up again and buffeted the vehicle, rocking it, making it feel like I was inside some lumbering beast.

CPS investigators use a lot of the same techniques as detectives. We need to get the facts, find out what happened, establish motive, understand why. Why. Why would Andrea crash the plane with her foster family on board? Why would she kill herself and throw everything away once her life finally seemed to be going right? Why?

Right now there was no answer. Not until Kaylee recovered a bit more. Maybe then she could fill in the gaping blanks. As such I was stalemated. Nothing left to do except my job.

———

Julia Roust's lawn was dead. Toys lay on their backs amid the brown blades like heatstroke victims. The house itself was neat and trim with what looked like a fresh coat of paint. The doorbell worked, gonging somewhere inside while I steadied myself on the front steps.

Part of a face peered at me through the little windows in the door. I gave my best reassuring smile, armor for what was to come, and said, "Julia?"

Julia Roust opened the door, and the next words caught in my throat.

You never get used to the residuals of violence. The debris in the wake of anger. You just recognize it quicker, can identify a bruise that shouldn't be where it is. We're taught in training that little kids' natural injuries are mostly focused around the head. It makes sense—their noggins are huge in proportion to their bodies. When they fall down, sometimes they can't keep from hitting their faces, splitting a lip, bruising an eyebrow. But as people age they get better at protecting themselves. Natural injuries tend to show up on hands, arms, knees, legs. Abuse reverses the natural order. It flows against gravity and winds up on the head again.

Julia Roust was walking proof.

Her eye was surrounded by mottled purple bruising bordering on black. The eye itself was bloodshot, and her ear on that side was so swollen it resembled an open car door. If I had to guess, the blow she took was a one and done. A quick, hard slap from the partner who typically followed it up with a *Look what you made me do* hook, or a *You know I love you* uppercut.

Julia looked at me watching her and tilted her head to one side. "Yeah?"

"Sorry. I'm Nora McTavish with child services."

"I already gave a statement to the cops."

"I know. I'm here to . . . may I come inside?"

"No. You may not." Julia punctuated this by stepping fully out onto the stoop. There wasn't a whole lot of room, so I retreated to ground level. In the full light of day I saw Julia was pretty. In spite, or because of, the injuries, her other features stood out in almost regal definition. And there was something in the way she held herself. Pride. She was proud. "What's this about?" she asked, crossing her arms. "My kid is fine."

"I understand that." Here was the cliff's edge again. Here was me stepping off it. No parachute. "I'm here in regard to the time period during the incident when your son was unsupervised."

Julia blinked. She half glanced over her shoulder, brow wrinkling in confusion. Then it dawned on her, full recognition setting into her jaw muscles, drawing down her eyebrows, sparking in her eyes. "Are you joking?"

I held up one hand. "First off, this is a technicality. I know what the situation—"

"The situation was he forced me into his fucking car and drove away with me," Julia said, cutting me off. She pointed to her injured face, bending closer to make sure I had a good look. "That was after he did this and said if I didn't want any more, I'd go with him."

"Julia, I think you did the right thing. You did the only thing you could."

"But you're still here to . . . what? Take my boy away? Because his father is crazy and violent and can't seem to understand we don't want anything to do with him?"

"You didn't file a restraining order," I said.

She looked away as if searching for something down the block. The wind came up and tugged a bit of her hair across her battered face, and she swiped it away with a finger. "Do you know what he told me? He said if I ever try to run from him or take his son away, he'll kill me. And I believe him. So no, I didn't file a restraining order because he'd walk right through it and slit my throat."

"It doesn't matter if you file an order or not, the district attorney is pressing charges on behalf of the state. He can't come within five hundred feet of you. He's in jail right now, and if he's convicted—"

"They'll lock him up forever?" she asked, taking a step closer and lowering her voice as if we were coconspirators. "Will they throw away the key? Is that the sentence for hitting your child's mother? No? Well, if I file a restraining order or testify against him, when he gets out I can tell you what he'll do. He'll probably go to his brother's, pick up a gun, and come hunt me down."

"Mom?"

The door had opened behind her. A boy, Sam, his name was—I had it in my file—stepped out onto the stoop. He was seven with bright, observant eyes, eyes that said he was used to recognizing trouble or threats, and they were locked on me now.

"Go back inside, honey," Julia said.

"Your soup is getting cold."

"Put it in the microwave for me."

Sam retreated. I gave him as reassuring a smile as I could. He didn't return it. The door shut.

I was shrinking. Had been since the moment I saw Julia's face. The same question that had surfaced after driving to the hospital rose again.

What was I doing here?

The envelope in my hand was thin, but so heavy I almost couldn't hold it out. "For what it's worth, I don't agree with the state statute, but you've been put on a probatory period. The details are inside."

Julia snatched the envelope from me. The anger had receded from her features like a passing storm. Now there was only resigned disgust. "Yeah, sure. Put me on probation when he'll be out on bail in twenty-four hours. And that restraining order you were talking about probably looks a whole lot like this." She waved the envelope. "A lot of good it will do us." She turned to go inside but paused. "You people. You come and talk about laws and statutes, but what do you really do to help? You're almost as bad as the bastard who did this." She gestured at her face, then snapped the door closed.

———

We're all to blame.

Someone once said we don't have a justice system, we have a legal system. I think about that.

I think about that a lot.

10

Nature versus nurture.

That catchy little alliteration, with the *versus* in the middle being the most important part of the phrase because it implies a debate is still open. That there's still hope.

On one side we have John Locke and a blank slate, which feels good, right? That idea we're all empty pages waiting to be written with the events of our lives and the reactions to those events. That we're in control. Then on the other we have Mr. Darwin and that pesky pre-determination of genes evident everywhere in nature, and that maybe doesn't give us a whole lot of confidence, does it? Like, say if your father was a sociopath who eventually was nudged into the land of full-blown psychopathy after your mother checked out on a permanent vacation? Say he took a high-powered rifle with a really expensive scope mounted to it and went to the top of the building he worked in and set up a little sniper's nest there. For the sake of conversation let's discuss the fact he sat there in the morning sunlight and shot coworker after coworker as they started showing up for the workday.

You tell me how important that *versus* would become.

I thought about this every time I walked into my brother's business and saw him standing behind the counter helping some impatient customer with their caffeine addiction—Stephen's patient and placid features like looking back in time to when our father was still alive. Same hairline, same nose, same jaw. But in every way that really mattered, they were different.

I was so thankful for that *versus*.

Stephen had opened the coffee shop three years ago with a loan from the small-business association. Initially it hadn't made sense to me, then it had. In the way I enjoyed open spaces and avoided small enclosures, Stephen liked people. He enjoyed the buzz of conversation, the shift of clothing and nonchalance of casual environments. The smell of coffee. Those sounds and stimuli were about as far as you could get from a tiny stinking closet with soiled blankets and hunger and darkness.

People aren't always ruled by their pasts, but they never really escape them either.

Stephen spotted me and he winked, holding up a couple fingers. *Two seconds.* Watching my brother serve customers their drinks and call out orders to his staff was like meditation for me. I zoned at the far end of the shop until he detached himself from the bar and made his way to my table, carrying two tall cups.

"Double mocha with whip," he said, setting down my drink.

"I told you I'm not having these anymore," I said, pulling the cup toward me.

"*Pah.* You can indulge."

"My jeans say otherwise."

"That's why they make larger sizes."

I clinked his glass with mine. "This is why I love you."

We drank and settled into our trademarked comfortable silence, surrounded by the din of the shop. Outside traffic trundled by, the sun appearing and receding, wind bending the branches of the nearest trees. Sitting there across from my brother was really the only place in the world I felt truly comfortable. He'd lived through the same things I had. We were tuned in to each other as much as two human beings could be, the shared trauma our specific radio channel.

"Busy," I said after a while.

"Yeah. This first real cold snap always brings them in. An excuse, but I'll take it. Do you ever notice how people use excuses to do what they really want?" I did. "The day I look out the window and find a reason for wanting another glass of wine or to jerk off is the day you need to put a bullet in my head à la the father express."

If someone knew our history they would've been aghast at Stephen's blasé dark humor. But it was a coping mechanism, like a child's blanket or a drunk's bottle.

I huffed a quiet laugh. "Or both at the same time."

Stephen's eyebrows shot up. "Cheers to that."

The quiet again between us. Then Stephen said, "Haven't seen much of you lately. Been spending more time in that cop's custody?"

"Some. Not as much as he'd like."

"Oh? Getting a little too close for comfort?"

"Something like that."

"Well, if you ever give him too much of the cold shoulder, tell him my door's always open."

"Will do." I picked at a napkin. Even Stephen's attempts to buoy me out of myself weren't working. He must've noticed because he reached across the table and stilled my fidgeting with a hand.

"Wanna tell me what's up?"

"No." He waited. Stephen's patience was astounding. I'd once watched him make a latte for a suburban mom four times until she finally declared the flavor correct. While I'd been trying not to reach for her throat, he never blinked. "I've been thinking about Paul," I said finally. Stephen only nodded. He didn't talk about Paul; it was the one subject where joking was verboten. Paul was part of his silence. "There was this boy who reminded me of him. The way he spoke and how—" I tried reconciling why Mason Roberts had reminded me so much of my brother. "He had the same dignity. Like he was above the hand he'd been dealt."

"What happened to him?" Stephen asked.

"He died." I drank a long swallow of coffee. "And I didn't . . ." I shook my head, not able to finish the thought. It was all so selfish. So menial in the grand scheme. Mason was dead, along with his foster siblings, and here I was trying to resolve the fact I hadn't stopped it from happening. Nothing would bring him back. Nothing would change what happened. Kids died every day, and the world spun on. Who the hell did I think I was?

"You know," Stephen said slowly, "when you told me you were going into social services, I thought, 'Great, perfect, it'll suit her.' Then you said you were going to work in child protection, and I thought, 'Oh, okay, this is about us.' And it is. But it's also just you." Stephen squeezed my hand he was still holding. "You want to help, simple as that. It's who you are. You've always wanted to help."

I looked out the window again. "I want to know. There's a difference."

———

He followed me onto the sidewalk when our coffees were gone. The line of customers had thinned, and a couple of his baristas were leaning against counters, scrolling on their phones. The wind shoved at us, and Stephen hunched his shoulders. "When's the last time you were out on your board?"

Surfing. I'd taken it up almost a decade ago in my midtwenties. The openness of the ocean and the solitary nature of the sport called to me. It was a private affair between you and the waves. Like a lone parishioner at church.

"I don't know. A few weeks," I said. "Water's getting cold."

"Never stopped you before." When I didn't answer, he said, "Well, if you don't go out on the water, you should go home to that lovely house of yours, draw a bath, open some wine, and soak."

"Do nothing then."

"Doing nothing is always doing something."

Stephen gave me a smile, and his never failed to make me return one of my own. I hugged him as if he were the older sibling. When I released him, he held me by the shoulders, studying me like a child who's fallen down. "You'll go home and rest?"

"I will."

"Good. Still coming to the little soirée on Saturday?"

"Wouldn't miss it."

He grinned. "Call me later. I'll fill you in on my last date. It was a fucking disaster."

I left him on the sidewalk and waved as I drove by. From what I could tell, he didn't seem to notice I was headed in the opposite direction of home.

11

Influencers for the most part adore their followers because they are numbers.

Those little numerals under a video or at the bottom of a blog saying how many people love you. They're pain blockers, dopamine hits; they're a drug for the creator. They are digital endorphins, not human beings with feelings and aspirations and lives of their own. Influencers want money and praise and adoration, or even to be hated. Not true connection. Not firsthand interaction.

That's why the most popular stars of the online community keep their addresses secret.

Because who wants user Net0696969 showing up at your house and asking for your fingernail clippings or for you to autograph your used feminine products they fished out of your trash?

Kaylee Volk was no different. In all the years she'd been growing her following, she took special care not to reveal her family's exact location. No shots outside their house with any identifying landmarks, no mentions of what school the kids attended or what gym she went to. If someone really wanted to find the Volks, they could. Anything was possible in this day and age. But it would take time and money and patience. And who had all three of those these days?

Lucky for me, I had an ID and authority.

The neighborhood the Volks lived in was on the western edge of the city, a fashionable section that used to be the oldest part of town when it was only an outpost settlement. Given this history the streets were narrow but flawlessly maintained, and old-growth trees towered over wide manicured lawns. By the time I rolled to a stop in front of the Volk residence, it was nearing dark, the last strands of sunset unraveling on the horizon. Up and down the street foreign cars shone in paved drives, but there was no one outside. Maybe it was passé to be caught on your lawn after dinner.

The Volks' home was two stories, a full porch lining the front level. Multiple eaves and dormers inlaid with dark windows. A front walk light glowed LED bright, casting faint shadows on the grass.

What was I doing here?

The time before evening fell had been spent driving around, seeing everything and nothing at once. Aimlessly knowing exactly where I was going. For some reason the Volk residence called and wouldn't let me go home. I needed to see it, to stand in its shadow the way kids might dare one another to approach the local haunted house.

Before climbing out of the car, something interesting caught my attention: a short way down the block a police cruiser idled. Behind the drapes of the Volks' front windows, a shape moved, and the door opened, casting a wedge of light onto the porch.

It's amazing how quickly our minds can calculate, how fast they can work to get us out of trouble. Or into it.

I was rounding my car's fender and heading up the walk, already reaching for my trusty ID when I realized I wouldn't need it. Instead I readied a load of bullshit. The officer standing on the front porch watching my approach was young and had a familiar face. More than familiar. He was a rookie named Tom Nelson, and at one point only a few short weeks ago, he'd been so drunk Byron had called him an Uber to take him home after he'd vomited off my back deck.

"Hi, Tom," I said, moving up the Volks' steps without pausing. It took him longer to realize who I was, but then all pretense of public servant versus civilian dropped. His posture relaxed, and his hand, which had been hovering near his duty belt and weapon, fell to his side.

"Nora, hey! What are you doing here?"

What was I doing here?

"Just need to do a walk-through to finish up some paperwork. They had an incident a couple of months back with the kids, and we want to make sure the, uh, crash wasn't a direct outcome." An internal wince tried climbing onto my face, but I forced it down.

Tom squinted a little, then shrugged. "Sure, I was heading out. A neighbor called and said they thought they saw someone skulking around. Checked everything, and the house is secure. Investigators already finished up too."

"Gotcha. I can lock up when I leave." I was stepping through the threshold, hoping the reason for being here didn't sound as thin as I thought it did when Tom spoke again.

"Uh, Nora?"

Shit. "Yeah?"

A downcast look had crept into Tom's eyes. He glanced at his boots. "Wanted to say again how sorry I am for the other night. Booze got the better of me. Normally I don't drink like that."

Heaving sigh of relief.

"No worries, Tom. We've all been there."

Tom's grin lit his whole face and he nodded. "Yeah, guess so. Okay, well, I'll see you later. Be sure to lock up."

"Will do."

He made his way down the walk and didn't look back. I shut the door.

Silence. The peaceful suburban quiet you pay a lot for. Before, it might've been pleasant when a family lived here, but now with the knowledge four out of five of them would never cross the threshold again, it made the skin crawl.

The entry led to a family room, which led to a kitchen wide and deep enough to play soccer in. Copper pots and pans hung from a rack over an island topped with threaded granite. Everything was clean. All the surfaces shone even in the low light. I moved through the room, touching the backs of chairs, placemats, countertops. Like they could say something, tell some story that hadn't been in any of Kaylee's videos.

A backpack hung from a kitchen chair. The zipper was open. Inside were T-shirts, shorts, and something flat and rectangular. A paperback—*The October Country*, Ray Bradbury. I saw Mason sitting across from me, saying it was just a fight, something stupid. Saying they were over it, everything was fine. Lying.

Book back in bag. Moving on.

A sitting room opened off the back of the house, revealing great views of a spacious and privately wooded backyard. It was darker beneath the trees, all of them swaying in the heavy wind, seeming to lean in and accuse, to ask a question. *What are you doing here?*

What was I doing here?

Laundry room, bathroom, then back in the family room where a large framed picture hung. It was all of them in matching outfits—jeans and white T-shirts—the kind of family picture that made me nervous on some elemental level. All of the Volk tribe was smiling, except Andrea. Beside the photo a stairway climbed to the second floor.

At the top of the stairs a long hallway ran in both directions, doors yawning open on either side. The wood floor creaked, and my hand swept out to flip on a light, but I pulled it back. I wasn't supposed to be here. No authority to search the house no matter what my little ID said. *Invading* was a good word. *Wrong* was a better one.

The first door opened to a quaint bathroom. Nothing out of the ordinary except what was in the trash. A crumpled fist of paper towels streaked with red. Blood. Not a lot, but there. They looked fairly fresh—within the last day or so for sure. Maybe something, maybe nothing. Hard to say. I moved on.

The next was too dark to see but flared fluorescent pink and yellow when I had no choice but to turn on a light. Bethany's room, then. Toys and clothes scattered here and there—a child's middle finger to the rest of the orderly house below. Posters of pop stars and animals on the wall. An unmade bed never to be made or slept in again. That was enough. Light off.

The next room was Mason's, the order and cleanliness and abundance of books as good as seeing his name written on the wall. The books here were a broader array than Bradbury, much broader. Stephen Hawking, Stephen King, Shakespeare, Keats, Frost. Books on the civil war and the first space programs. Books regarding clean energy and early Mesopotamian sculpture. The kid seemed interested in everything. There were no dirty clothes anywhere but in the hamper, no dust bunnies under the bed. A line of shoes so straight you could measure by them beside a desk.

Pens and pencils and paper in the desk drawers. And college pamphlets. Lots of them. It looked like a collection. Like other people collect bottle caps or stamps, Mason collected good schools from all across the country. I started going through the glossy university pamphlets with all the smiling teenagers and flawless campus grounds, and suddenly they were too heavy. It was worse seeing these than Bethany's unmade bed. These dreams of a future that would never arrive.

The room across the hall was Andrea's.

The smell was the first thing that hit me. A waft of shampoo and some expensive perfume. A little too potent. The room itself overlooked the back lawn. Below the tall windows the sitting room's roof slanted away to a gutter peppered with leaves. Her bed was made, and an outfit—shredded jeans and a tank top—was strewn on the comforter. A few more items of clothing spilled out from an open closet, trailing toward a drafting desk.

On the desk's canted surface were pages of drawing paper, different sizes, all piled together. An array of pencils and erasers sat in the tray. It took almost a minute for the drawings to make sense, to reconcile them with the girl with the ratty clothes and fuck-you eyes.

They were fashion design sketches, stunning in their vibrant elegance. Stylish dresses and chic skirts. Trendy and cute blouses and smart business suits. Most were women's styles, but there were drawings of men's clothing, too, along with some kids'. It was transfixing. My fingers paged through the art over and over, drinking in the clean and casual lines, the subtle but undeniable talent. One of the last drawings seemed to be fashion for what you'd call a "tween," and written along its edge was, *To Bethy, thanks for being my model!*

Sometimes the heart hides. It hides in our dreams, our words, our passions. Andrea's was hidden here in these drawings. She'd had a real flair for elegant fashion beneath a calloused exterior. In the desk's only drawer was a single piece of paper—much larger than the other sketch pages and thicker, more tangible. Andrea had even thrown a little color in between the bold pencil lines.

It was the front of a boutique clothing shop. The windows were mocked up with sprawling models in Andrea's fashion stylings, and a sign over the door read PARISHUNLTD.

More dreams cut off before they could flourish.

But why?

I hovered over the pages. Scanned through them again, touching each as I'd touched the items in the kitchen, waiting for them to tell a story. Tell me why this talented young woman had hurt Mason. Why she'd killed herself and most of her family.

When there was no answer apparent, I turned to leave, stopping for a second to study an overstuffed purple teddy bear sitting on a futon in the corner of the room. "You know why?" I asked it, hoping my voice would break the frustrated tension, but it only sounded flat and out of place in the quiet.

The last door at the far end of the hall was the main bedroom. As the door swung inward it revealed a spacious area taken up mostly by what could only be a California king bed. Matching bedside tables and lamps. A large dresser along one wall. A walk-in closet that could've rented out for a thousand a month in New York. An en suite bathroom. Spotless.

I stood there the longest, turning in a slow circle, looking at the walk-in shower, the double vanity, the toilet, the large medicine cabinet in the center of it all—the last being the most interesting. Because that's really the subconscious of most households, right? The place where all the secrets are kept, the insecurities, the ugly truths.

Except this one was glaringly boring. Toothpaste. Deodorant. Mouthwash. Aspirin. Cough medicine. An over-the-counter sleep aid with only a few pills missing. Nothing damning. My hand lingered on the mirrored door, then pushed it closed. As I was about to move back into the bedroom, something beneath the sinks caught my eye. Garbage cans. His and hers.

One, Kaylee's since it was beneath her vanity, was empty. The other, not quite. At the very bottom among two used Q-tips was a pill bottle. An unmarked pill bottle with nothing inside except a faint chalky smell.

A thud came from downstairs.

I froze, listening, trying to hear past the sound of the wind and my heartbeat. Waiting. Nothing. Had I locked the front door after Tom left? Yes. Definitely. All at once the gravity of where I was pressed down. Not only the inappropriateness of it, but the haunting weight of the empty house where only ghosts lived now. It was time to go.

I considered taking the pill bottle with me, but ultimately there was nothing more to glean from it, and it went back in the trash. As I came out of the bathroom the light caught something on the wall above the dresser that hadn't stood out before. From this angle it was quite noticeable. A sizeable dent in the sheetrock. Closer up, it was apparent something had hit it with substantial force, the wall broken and leaking dust when touched. Not a fist, it was too high above the dresser for someone to have struck it effectively. No, maybe something thrown.

The need to exit the house and the compulsion to keep looking tug-of-warred until I finally stepped forward and pushed the side of my head tight to the wall, looking into the narrow space behind the dresser.

There was something down there.

You can go home. Not all is lost. This family's tragedy isn't your fault. You have your own tragedy; you don't need theirs too. Just walk away.

The dresser came away from the wall easily enough, and what was behind it tipped and fell flat.

An iPad.

And not just any iPad. This one had a decorative case, thick and rubbery, in the colors of pink and yellow. A kid's iPad. Its screen was black and shattered and stayed that way when I picked it up and tried turning it on. A blinded eye. White dust coated one corner of the protective case and when placed into the dent in the wall, it fit like a key in a lock.

What might've been the wind shifting the house or a footstep in the hall came from behind me.

I spun, clutching the device to my chest, half expecting someone to be framed in the doorway, but it was empty. The wind shoved hard at the building again and hissed around the windows. The time to leave had been ten minutes ago. Retrospectively, never coming here would've been the better choice. Either way it was time to go.

A second later the dresser was back in place, and I was in the hall. It was empty and quiet. The light had dimmed even more, and now the shadows were deep. Was it colder in here? No, just my imagination. A case of the heebie-jeebies. A sign that reason had come and gone and that the jittery bird of panic had awakened and was flapping its wings in your head.

The stairway seemed too distant, as if the hall had lengthened while I hadn't been looking. Eight steps, maybe nine. Just go. Go.

One step.

Two.

Three.

Four.

A flicker of movement came from the left, and my stomach clenched, seizing so hard it hurt. What was it? Nerves? There was nothing there, just the hallway and doors, some closed, others open. Like Andrea's.

Had I closed Andrea's door?

My mouth was chalk dry, and I thought of the rasping sound Kaylee's tongue had made across her stitches. "Hello?" I said quietly.

There was a screech from Andrea's room, and her door slammed shut.

I fell back against the wall, legs trying to run, heart thundering. A few muted thumps came from Andrea's room, then nothing. Just the sound of the wind and cold air gusting into the hall. Coming from beneath her door.

We become passengers sometimes. We like to think we're in control and the electrically charged tissue in our heads is the captain steering the ship. But sometimes an iceberg comes out of the fog, and evasive measures are taken. We're suddenly the people holding on for dear life, hoping whoever's driving knows what the fuck they're doing.

That was what it felt like walking to the closed door, reaching out a hand that didn't feel attached to my body to turn the knob. Looking inside the bedroom, expecting an axe to come hurtling out of the dark and bury itself in my foolish skull.

But instead there was just a room. A room belonging to a girl who used to be good at running away and was better at drawing beautiful clothes. A room, cold now because one of the windows was wide open, the curtain billowing inward. Past the window was the short roof of the room below, and beyond that the empty darkened yard.

Leaving the house was a blur. Shutting the window, hurrying down the hallway, down the stairs. Struggling with the two locks on the front door before managing to get out. Then along the walk to the car, glancing back every few steps, and inside. Safe. Safer.

Two things registered as I drove away, unable to put distance between me and the house fast enough. The first was I'd taken the iPad with me. The placating voice in your head telling you it was only panic, you'd only held on to the device because you hadn't realized you were holding it, so easy to listen to. So easy to believe. The truth was you probably always planned on taking it. There was no other choice.

And the second didn't make sense. Someone had been in the house with me, had gone into Andrea's room and escaped through the window before I could see who it was. And of all the things to take, why take what was missing?

Why take the big purple teddy bear?

12

Update | Kaylee Volk

85,144 views * Oct 14, 2022

Kaylee Volk (Volks At Home)

789K SUBSCRIBERS

UPDATE ON CONDITION A heartfelt thank you.

Video Plays

No upbeat music or graphics frame the start of the video. Just Kaylee in a hospital bed. Dark bruises cover her face, masklike. Her hair is lank, and deep bags hang beneath her eyes. She smiles sadly, wearily.
KAYLEE
(voice gravelly, unused)
Hey, everyone.
(long pause)

I don't know how to begin a post like this. It's—
(tears flood her eyes as she looks off-screen)
You've heard the news. My family—

Her face crumples with emotion, and she turns the camera away for a moment before continuing.
KAYLEE
(more composed)
I just wanted to say thank you for the outpouring of support. Your kindness is amazing, and it's what's keeping me going. I'm . . . I'm doing as well as I can. I'm healing, but . . . nothing's ever going to be the same.
(tearing up again)
I'll post again when I can, but that's all I can say for now.

Video Ends

13

Paul watched me from across the street.

Between flashes of traffic his fading face was there, obscure and utterly recognizable. I sat in my car with the windows up against the mist struggling to be rain.

I'd spent the morning in court and was still recovering. Court was the vampire of our profession. Its density of unvarnished facts drained you. A seemingly unending parade of familial anguish you were sometimes called to weigh in on in the most detached and clinical manner. That legal language we used couldn't convey the true weight of what we were discussing—literally deciding people's fates. But we did it anyway. We tried. We all tried. Though at times when no one was asking me to make a statement or a lull fell over the proceedings, I'd glance around, take in everything as it was and wonder, *Is this the best we can do? Really?*

We're all to blame.

Paul blended into a group of people crossing the street and was gone. I sat for a beat in the courthouse parking lot, rewinding first through the morning hours, then the night before.

The iPad was broken. Really broken. It wouldn't charge, wouldn't turn on, wouldn't anything. Any hope to glean why someone had hurled it at a wall was dashed just as the device had been. Byron had texted, and I'd ignored his query as to whether I was home or not. I also let two of his calls this morning go to voice mail. Alone had been preferable.

The idea of talking to anyone after being in the Volk house was out of the question. They would've heard it in my voice, known something was wrong. Merrill had brought me back down to earth with his calm gaze and soft fur. That and two brimming glasses of wine.

The exploration of the house felt like a dream now. Some ill-remembered fog harboring a blade of fear. Someone had been there, had been in the next room. Had maybe stood behind me watching at some point. The thought brought goose bumps even in the early-afternoon storm light. Who had been there, and why? I didn't like where this line of thinking was headed.

The thoughts lulled me, put me into a trance I snapped free of with the rap of knuckles on the driver's window.

Byron. He smiled his white, even smile, hands shucked into his rain jacket. "Hey," he said as the window went down.

"Hey."

"Did you get my texts?"

"Yeah. Was in court all morning," I said, gesturing at the building behind him.

"Oh, right. Where were you last night? I stopped by, but you weren't around."

"You stopped by?" Too much of an edge to the question for him not to notice.

"Yeah, I mean, I was just swinging through." He looked guilty of something even though he wasn't. I was. And it made me angry.

"I was out."

"Okay." He glanced away for a second, and I hoped he'd let it drop. He didn't. "So what's up with you?"

"Nothing."

"Nothing seems like something."

"I just don't need you coming by every night, that's all."

He blinked like I'd struck him. "Right. Right."

"Sorry. That came out wrong."

"Did it?"

"I'm a little stressed, that's all."

The rain started to get more serious about falling. Byron didn't seem to notice. "The Volk thing."

"Yeah."

"You really need to let it go." I looked away, studying a gull picking at a piece of garbage across the parking lot until Byron released a long sigh and started away. He glanced over his shoulder once and said, "Check your voice mail when you get a minute."

Then he was unlocking his patrol car and climbing inside. I rolled up the window and watched him pull away.

Byron. Good, sweet, well-hung Byron. This man who meant no harm, who knew how to cook and of the many cops I'd known, held true public service in his heart. He might've been born with a birthmark in the shape of a badge. I went back to meeting him the first time in court, how he hadn't condescended regarding the case in question, was only helpful and polite. And when he'd asked me out for a drink later, it had been casual, no big thing. Which was partially why I said yes in the first place. But lately when we were together, it felt like I was being wrapped tighter and tighter inside the folds of a soaking blanket. Being waterboarded with affection. The stifling sense of nearness made me want to claw my skin off. And yet, I really liked the guy.

He'd left one message that morning while I was in court, his voice faint at first on the recording, then clearer. "Hey, it's me. I know you're really upset about the Volks, but I didn't want you to hear it anywhere else first. The youngest girl's body washed in this morning. Bethany. Knew you'd want to know. Call me if you want to talk."

My eyes stared back from the rearview mirror, and I gave it a twist so it faced the car's roof. That hollow space inside you that's like a cave. A bolt hole you can retreat into when things are too much. I let myself go there, trying not to picture the little girl's room, her unmade bed and toys forever waiting for her to return.

When there was a semblance of control again, I found the address I'd tapped into my phone early that morning at work. The address lifted from Andrea Parish's file.

I could go back to work, move on to the next case—God knew there were enough of them—keep fighting the good fight. I could do that. I *should* do that for my own sake and everyone else's.

Or I could try to quiet the sound of trickling water in the back of my mind. I could try shutting off the leaking faucet.

I put the car in drive and pulled out of the parking lot as it began to rain in earnest.

———

Foster children share a lot in common with convicts. They've both been taken in and processed by the state. Both placed in environments and situations not of their choosing. And both have "rap sheets" in that their crimes, or someone else's, have been listed, recorded. A life whittled down to misdeeds and subjections. These rap sheets also include family, friends, and known associates.

Taylor Waylan was one such associate of Andrea's. Eighteen going on nineteen going on forty, Taylor had been in the same foster family as Andrea prior to her placement with the Volks. They'd become friends, Andrea even listing the older girl as her emergency contact in the school registry. Taylor had originally been placed in foster care after her mother died in a traffic accident and her father was deemed unfit to care for her at the time. After turning eighteen she moved in with him, and from what could be gleaned, began looking after an ailing alcoholic with paranoid delusions.

Which elevated the stakes of walking up and knocking on their front door. No one answered after a few minutes, and I retreated to the car. A stakeout then. Yet another investigative tactic. I was becoming a regular Columbo. Add a rumpled raincoat and some cigars, and I'd be set.

The office number appeared on my cell. Silenced. Probably Kelly wondering where I was. Wondering what I was doing.

What *was* I doing here?

It was one thing to visit a parent from a former inquiry. Quite another to enter their home and take their possessions. To stake out a woman's home to ask her questions about her dead friend. For the record I wasn't angry with Byron because he was wrong. Letting this go was the right thing to do. But the right thing didn't always help you sleep at night.

In the end it wasn't a long wait. Taylor appeared on the farthest street corner, moving briskly through the rain beneath an umbrella. She wore a waitressing uniform, black slacks and a white frilly blouse with the name tag still attached. She was pretty in a severe way with short, dark hair and eyes to match. The edge of a tattoo peeked from the collar of her shirt and crawled halfway up her neck. When she was almost to her door, I hurried up the walk behind her.

"Taylor?"

She spun, keys poking out of her fist. Good girl. "Yeah?"

"I'm Nora. I'm with child protective services."

"Yeah?"

"I was wondering if I could talk to you about Andrea."

She stiffened. "She's dead. What's there to talk about?"

"A lot, I think."

"You think." There was sad laughter in the two words. Taylor seemed to consider it, then nodded toward the house. "Better now, I guess. Dad's out somewhere. You wouldn't want to be here when he's home."

She unlocked the door and we went inside.

The house smelled like someone had tried to clean up and failed over and over again. That flowery canned scent not really pulling its weight, all the smells beneath crawling out. Old cigarettes and body odor. Sweat and maybe a cat, maybe not. There was clutter, but things were clean. It looked like Taylor's hours didn't end when she left work; they just paused until she could come home and begin tidying whatever her father had gotten up to while she was out.

Magazines were stacked against one wall of the living room, most covers emblazoned with guns positioned like some sort of sex objects. A folding table overflowed with electronics and soldering tools. Dishes were piled in the kitchen, but they looked fresh enough. Two empty vodka bottles stood near the sink. Taylor busied herself in the cabinets, and after a minute the smell of coffee overrode whatever else had baked itself into the house's carpet and walls.

"Want a cup?" she asked.

"No. Thanks, though."

She appeared a second later holding a brimming mug and gestured toward the living room. I settled onto an ancient love seat, which squealed in protest, and Taylor dropped into a recliner opposite. As I was arranging my thoughts I noticed a handgun lying on the coffee table between us. Taylor saw me looking and sat forward, tossing an old newspaper over it.

"My dad leaves his shit everywhere." She sipped her drink and looked away.

"Where do you work?" I said, motioning to her name tag.

"A café named Herald's. Nothing but class."

"Full time?"

She laughed. "And pay benefits? No. I work a night shift at a gas station a few times a week to fill the gap."

"Two jobs. That's a lot. College, too, or—?"

"Nope."

"So—"

"Listen, the cops already stopped by. I told them what I had to say."

"Which was?" Taylor shrugged. I waited, but she said nothing else, just watched me. "You and Andrea were close." Another shrug. "Did she say anything to you prior to the crash?"

"Like what?"

"Like anything."

"What does it matter? Why are you here?"

Moment of half truth. "There was an incident last month. Andrea and Mason got in a fight. She choked him. Did you know about that?"

"No. But it doesn't surprise me. She had a temper."

Andrea did it.

"Did the two of you ever fight?"

"No. We understood each other. I knew enough not to piss her off."

I absorbed this. "Was she using drugs?"

"Oh yeah, tons. All the time," she deadpanned. When I only looked at her and waited, she said, "Not any more than anyone else."

"Was anything bothering her?"

Taylor hesitated. She looked around, then leaned forward, found an open pack of cigarettes, and lit up. Puffing, she said, "You want to know about Andrea? She was always looking for something better, something else. She hated that goddamn scar her dad gave her. Hated it was there every time she looked in the mirror. That's what she was running from. She wanted more than she was."

"Like her clothing designs."

Taylor's eyes shot up to mine. "She told you about her designs?"

"She mentioned it when we talked." My control of the conversation was slipping. Taylor was looking at me like an animal that had been tricked before and wouldn't be cornered again, one getting ready to run.

"Really. She never even showed her sketches to me."

Shit. "I don't think she meant to tell me. It slipped out." Evasive maneuvers required. "Was she happy with the Volks?"

Taylor stabbed her smoke out and finished her coffee. "I guess. Her foster mom drove her nuts with the whole influencer thing."

"Why didn't she move out? She was eighteen."

"With what money? She didn't have a job. Whenever we went somewhere, I had to pay." There was petty acid in her tone. Taylor seemed to hear it, too, and her voice softened. "She just had to put up with it until . . ."

"Until what?"

"Until she graduated."

I let the silence of the house close in for a second. Kept watching her. "Was Andrea seeing someone?"

"Not really. No."

"Not really, or no?"

"There was a guy. No one else knew about him."

"Who was he?"

"I don't know, some guy. Never met him."

The lie hung heavy in the air for a beat. "Did her foster parents know she was seeing someone?"

Taylor barked laughter, then covered her mouth. "No. They were kinda strict. She had to sneak out sometimes if we wanted to hang. Andrea didn't really trust Kaylee."

"Why?"

"She's got issues."

"Like?"

"Baggage. Andrea said she was fucked up from her childhood. She put everything on her YouTube channel trying to be 'the perfect family.'" Taylor threw air quotes with her fingers.

"You don't think they were?"

She studied me, maybe wondering if I was serious or not. "There's no such thing."

———

Taylor followed me onto the front steps as I left. This girl, barely an adult, working two jobs to care for a father in all the ways he'd failed to care for her. Giving up some of her future, maybe all of it, to help someone else bent on self-destruction. This product of the system with her tattoos and anger covering up a deeper sadness, doing the very best she could with what she had. Given where we stood Julia Roust came to mind, and I realized the two women weren't far apart in age.

We forget how young some people are when they start carrying weight beyond their years, then wonder why they struggle.

I dug in my purse and handed her one of my business cards. "That's my cell on there. I answer day or night. You think of anything or just need to talk, call me." Taylor responded with a tight smile, and I turned to go but paused. "I'm really sorry about Andrea. I know how tough it is losing someone close." A tremor went through her expression, threatened to crack the mask and let the sorrow slip out. But just as quickly it was shored up, and she shut the door.

The rain had tapered off and pinged in puddles erratically, sending out concentric ripples. Inside the car it was dry and warm and quiet. Thoughts traced their way through my head, creating ripples of their own.

Taylor knew more than she was saying, that was clear enough. Whether or not she would ever come out with the truth was hazy. For now I had to let her be. Julia Roust's face surfaced and submerged again, and something that had been floating free in the back of my mind clicked into place. A semblance of calm and rightness fell over me. I had a plan now, and it was always good to have one, even if it was shaky at best.

As far as the Volks went, I knew what I had to do next, and there was no time like the present.

14

CPS workers have a spectrum of questions they ask when investigating abuse or neglect cases.

They ask the parents about their own childhoods, about drinking, about current drug use, about watching porn. They ask about certain household routines, try to establish a pattern or back trail from their pasts that might lead to the abuse that's potentially going on now. Because humans are learning machines. We learn by what's done to us, not just what we're taught. We learn to injure and touch and wound what we shouldn't. We learn to abuse and abandon if we're hurt and lost. The past imprints on the future like a typewriter slowly running out of ink.

Justin Volk was mostly an open book—a rich kid from a rich family who grew up to work at his rich family's rich business. He followed the privileged bible to the point of triteness, traveling Europe during college and qualifying for his pilot's license shortly thereafter before settling down with Kaylee and beginning to work for daddy. There was at least one bookmark in his pages I'd need to return to, but that could come later. Right now Kaylee was my concern—as much as Justin's history was straightforward, hers was more complex.

Kaylee Volk was born Kaylee Baker, a middle child between a younger brother and an older sister. The family was upper class heading toward the 1 percent with her mother working as a successful independent film producer and her father as a Portland city auditor. They lived in a prestigious suburb surrounded by other equally ambitious and successful people. Perfect life, perfect family. That was, until a few months after Kaylee's twelfth birthday, when her father was indicted on embezzlement charges.

Cue the shattering of a suburban dream.

Alan Baker had been using taxpayer dollars to finance everything from his membership at the country club to some of his wife's clientele's films. Over $1 million in a five-year span. The court was not kind. Fifteen years minimum without possibility of early parole. Kaylee's mother, Clarice, was cleared of formal charges but bore the mark of scandal nonetheless. Her business crashed and burned, former colleagues nulled and voided their association. She began drinking and seeing one of her former assistants on the side. The kids were removed from their private school, and the Bakers left their sprawling suburban home for a three-bedroom apartment. But the fallout didn't end there.

A towel smuggled into Alan's cell cut his prison term short. Apparently he wasn't made for long-term confinement. Clarice took his suicide badly, drinking too many martinis at a friend's place one evening before attempting to drive home. Authorities thought she'd been doing close to eighty when her car left the interstate. A broken back and brain damage left her in a persistent vegetative state. She lived for a year that way before a stroke finished her off.

Cue state-mandated foster care.

With no close family the three kids were split up and moved a half dozen times before they'd become adults. Kaylee's younger brother, Evan, immersed himself in drugs to cope. First using, then selling. A second offense earned him three years in a state pen. He'd only been released the year before at the age of twenty-two. Natalie, Kaylee's older sister, seemed impervious to their family's tragedy. She graduated salutatorian from high school and went on to be accepted to the Royal

Academy of Dramatic Art in London. At twenty-eight she'd been cast in two feature films and was a steadily rising star.

While her brother plummeted and her sister ascended, Kaylee languished. Social service reports painted her as morose, unresponsive, unable to connect. She passed classes with straight Cs, joined no social clubs or sports, and dropped out of college after two semesters. The trajectory of her life appeared to change directly after meeting Justin—her first video being uploaded to YouTube shortly before accepting Bethany into their home. It garnered only a few thousand views, but slowly and surely her following grew with every upload.

Now I stared at the number listed beneath her profile, well over three-quarters of a million subscribers, and watched her make a brief and tearful thank you from her hospital bed. My viewing was one of nearly three hundred thousand, with more racking up by the hour. She was trending on other social media platforms, and one headline from a major news source promised an exclusive interview in the days to come.

Tragedy was a consumable commodity, and everyone was buying.

Slowly I clicked back through the half dozen or so tabs open on my work computer, which had told the family's story. Insight into the foster parents' background hadn't unlocked any doors in regard to the crash or what had caused Andrea to hurt Mason, but trying to understand everyone involved was crucial. You never knew what detail might resurface and clear the waters so you could see what was right before you.

Researching Kaylee's history had eaten up the better part of the afternoon, and my neck was filled with crushed glass from sitting in one position too long. Turning my head to the right produced a satisfying pop, cranking it to the left gave me a much less satisfying view of Jim Kelly's butt-ugly tie.

"What are you doing?" Kelly asked, an arm cocked on the top of the nearest cubicle wall.

"Working," I said, swiveling in the chair to face him.

He surveyed the YouTube video of Kaylee still pulled up on my screen. "Uh-huh."

"What did you need?" I asked, turning back to my desk. The way to deal with supervisors like Kelly was to appear inconvenienced by their presence, to seem as if they were obstructing work progress, since to them that was the most cardinal of sins.

"You didn't answer your phone earlier."

"I was in court. I figured if it was important you would've left a message."

"I wanted to make sure you served Julia Roust."

"Why wouldn't I?"

"You seemed averse to it leaving my office."

"Like you always say, Jim, we don't make the rules."

"Nora, I'm concerned."

Enough. I turned in my chair again. "Okay. What?"

"Your attitude lately hasn't been optimal."

"I didn't know 'optimal attitude' was a position requirement."

"You know what I mean. Your office decorum has been lacking."

I thought about Richard Jackson, Kelly's drinking buddy who sloughed off his workload every chance he got, and bit back my reply. Kelly was talking again, saying something about "pulling together," some metaphor about a boat and rowing, and I just nodded, eyes unfocusing. There comes a time in everyone's life where they begin wondering what the point is. If they're making a difference or just treading water. What was the point of work if it only funded a week's vacation in some paradise where you could only ever be a visitor, never a resident? What good was it to hate waking up on Monday morning only to yearn for Friday night? If purpose became a perk not a prerequisite, what the hell were we even doing?

What was I doing here?

"So I hope you think about that," Kelly finished.

"I certainly will," I said. He seemed satisfied. Mission accomplished.

When he'd meandered away to another cubicle, I placed a few calls, the last going to Julia Roust's voice mail. I hoped she'd get it and agree to what I was proposing.

The usual eager sounds of people departing came from every corner of the room. It was 5:00 p.m. on a Friday, time to get the hell out. On the way to the parking lot my thoughts drifted to Stephen's suggestion of going out on the water. The sky had cleared, and the air possessed more warmth than any other day in the last week. It might be my last chance to climb on a board before spring. But there was one more necessary stop prior to heading home. I hoped I was up to it. I hoped it wasn't a mistake.

15

Kaylee Volk wasn't in her hospital bed.

She wasn't in the bathroom, either, and just when I was about to return to the nurse's station to inquire if she'd been moved to a different room, Kaylee appeared in the doorway. The nurse who had booted me on my last visit was with her, steering a walker that doubled as a chair.

"Hi, Mrs. Volk, I hope I'm not disturbing you," I said, giving her, then the nurse, as sunny a smile as I could muster.

"Nora, right? No, not at all. Sit down."

The nurse's mouth pursed so tight, I thought it might actually disappear. "Kaylee, you should rest, especially after that walk."

"I'll be fine, Tina."

"You sure?"

"Yes."

Tina got Kaylee arranged in bed, then breezed past me without another glance. "She doesn't like me," I said when we were alone.

"She doesn't like visitors in general," Kaylee said with a wan smile.

"You're up and moving, that's good to see," I said, settling into a bedside chair.

"Necessary for recovery is what they tell me." Kaylee's face was even more colorful than in her latest video, the bruising a poisonous sunset across her features. "Sorry about the last time you stopped by. I was on a lot of painkillers."

"Don't apologize. I shouldn't have bothered you." We sat for a beat while I gathered my thoughts. As I opened my mouth to begin, Kaylee spoke instead.

"I think I know why you're here."

"You do?"

"You're worried you missed something, right? About Andrea?"

It was like I'd been struck. Was it that apparent? Was I a walking billboard of doubt? "I wanted—actually needed to gather some information for a report, since Andrea and Mason's incident was so close to their . . ." *Deaths*, I was going to say, but caught myself.

Kaylee nodded as if in a daze. For all appearances she might've still been in shock. Maybe she was. Maybe it was just drugs. "You were really kind when you interviewed us. Professional. I know Justin was upset the whole thing got brought up. He thought it was blown out of proportion." Kaylee swallowed thickly. "He was just embarrassed."

"You were both very cooperative," I said. "But yes, I was wondering if you could tell me anything more about Andrea's behavior that might explain why she—why she would do this."

Kaylee's brow drew together as she thought. "She was different the last few months. Strange."

"Strange how?"

"Remote. She wasn't eating as much. Angry." Kaylee looked down to her lap. "I didn't understand it. Thought it was a transition thing. Her becoming an adult. I don't know."

"Was there anything else? I spoke with one of her friends, and she mentioned a possible boyfriend. Was Andrea seeing anyone new or hanging out with different people?"

"Not that I can think of."

"You didn't notice anything else, anything that could've been drug related? Odd hours or other changes?"

A flicker of something crossed her eyes, there and gone. "I don't know. But there was something wrong with Justin. He—" She grimaced, swallowing again. "In the plane, after he took off, he was talking funny."

I leaned forward. "Funny how?"

"Slow. Slurry, kind of like he was drunk. That was when she . . ." Kaylee looked at me, and for a second I believed there'd been a mistake and she had died out there in the water. The person in the bed was a corpse, a shell of her former self with haunted pits where her eyes should be. "She was in the copilot seat, and she started pushing the controls down. Justin tried to stop her, but there was something wrong with him. Everyone was screaming. Oh God."

My stomach was a bundle of snakes, tight and slithering. "Listen, it's okay. You don't have to tell me any more." But it was like she was in a trance, her empty gaze focused on the opposite wall now.

"The water came up so fast, and there was nothing I could do. It was so fast. Then everything was black." Her throat worked, and she reached for something. It was a moment before I noticed the bedpan. I got it to her just in time. As Kaylee retched I poured a cup of water from the pitcher beside her bed. My hands shook. When she was finished being sick, she took a few sips and lay back against the pillows, her eyes drifting closed.

"I'm so sorry," I said.

Her voice was weak but insistent. "It's like a nightmare. I keep waking up and thinking I dreamed it. I wish . . . I wish I was with them." She faded for a beat, then came back, eyes opening to slits and finding me. "I wish I was dead too."

———

The water temp hovered around fifty degrees, cold enough to sting and numb but not cold enough to keep people from riding some of the

Joe Hart

better waves rolling into the coast this time of year. From the secluded cove the other surfers were only specks, miles to the south, boards and spray catching the last rays of sun. No one else had ventured down the little access lane leading to the rocky shore below my neighborhood. That was good. That was fine. Alone was better.

Merrill chuffed once as I donned my wet suit. He didn't like the look of me in it. Sometimes I chased him around after putting it on. Me taking big, long strides with my arms outstretched, him dancing away and woofing playfully—his head and shoulders lowered, ass up and wiggling in the air. Our little game. None of that today.

Merrill seemed to sense my mood and curled up in the roots of a tree overhanging the beach. He watched as his master lay on her board and paddled out, the motion rusty at first, then smoother. Past the breakers it was fairly calm. Calm enough to sit up and float, take in the coastline, hear the cries of gulls and people, feel the swell of each wave, gentle here before they climbed and rolled closer to shore.

There's a point in surfing when you have to commit. You've got your timing down, know the feeling of the coming swell and have paddled in the right distance. Then it's a matter of popping up onto the board and angling with how the wave is going to curl, feeling the inevitable power under your feet. Once you're there you're either going to ride it or fall. There's no going back; it's going to happen, one way or another.

It was how the last few days felt. I'd paddled out and a wave was coming. It was rising to my back. There was still time to stop. To not commit and let it go by, let it wash in without me. Because I was afraid. Afraid as soon as I stood up, I'd catch sight of the thing behind me, and it wouldn't be some ordinary wave, but a tsunami. No chance of conquering it, only of being plowed under by it. Consumed.

Consumed. For me that word had always been synonymous with the darkness that filled the closet where our father had locked us. It had been complete. All encompassing.

He'd kept us there for twenty-six days.

To this day I don't know why he kept us alive. Whether it was just part of his incomprehensible machinations, or if it was something else. Maybe his idea of mercy. I don't know, don't want to. But every so often the drill would hum, and the screws would retreat. The door would open briefly, and the dark would be broken for a moment. Some food and water would be slid inside. Then we'd be sealed up again. Tomblike. We used one corner of the six-by-eight-foot space as a bathroom. The air became noxious, our eyes stung from the ammonia even with Paul piling clothes on our waste. Hunger became our fourth companion in that little room. It took up residence inside us all and ate its fill. I imagined it as a white burning ball with claws like spades, digging deeper and deeper into my center until it felt as if it would tunnel out through my back. Stephen was only six at the time, and he cried a lot. Paul and I tried to comfort him, smoothing his hair like our mother used to do, giving him the thickest clothes to sleep on while Paul told us stories.

And gave us his share of food.

Stephen and I didn't know until the day of our rescue. Voices came first from out in the entry, low and cautious, then louder, calling our names. We barely had the strength to reply. It wasn't until they were breaking open the door that I realized it was only Stephen and I answering them.

The light was full of razor blades when the door finally opened. I heard someone say *Oh my God*, their voice so horrified it bordered on reverence. When I could see again, there were people kneeling in the doorway, kneeling over a bundle of sticks wrapped in Paul's clothes. Kneeling over my brother.

Later the doctors told us Paul had eaten very little of the food in that almost month-long imprisonment. He'd passed the rest to us. They said he'd probably died a few hours before social services arrived. As far as I was concerned they could've kept that bit of information to themselves.

Before we were taken away, before we learned what had become of our father and why the police and child services had descended upon our home that day—why there'd been no food or water in the last twenty-four hours or so—I picked up Paul's Saint Anthony medal. It had fallen from his hand as they lifted him from the closet floor. He'd been holding it instead of wearing it, maybe to keep himself from eating his share of the food because he knew if he did then we'd all die. That little silver medal with a saint of lost things imprinted on it.

But Paul was the saint, and we were the lost things, and he saved us. Helped us be found.

———

Gulls wheeled and screamed. The shore crashed with waves. I sat motionless in the deep water until the light slanted down and the sun extinguished itself in the Pacific.

Eventually I paddled in, feeling the water rise exponentially, accepted its challenge, and committed.

16

Famous people are hard to contact.

Once a person rises above a certain status point, they're no longer readily accessible to the rabble. They withdraw behind a protective wall of publicists and managers. They become paranoid, and for good reason. Being known and exposed to a large population is a statistics game. There are studies suggesting one in a hundred people are sociopaths. Really when you think about it, it's not hard to believe.

So when I placed a call to Kaylee's older sister, Natalie Baker—now Natalie Winston—it was met by a recording in her agent's office. *Please leave a message, and we'll return your call at the earliest convenience.* Right. I left one anyway. I didn't know the status of Kaylee and Natalie's relationship but thought maybe the older sister might have some insight into the family I hadn't been able to glean from the interviews or online. Anything to help. Anything to get a better handle on things.

It was early Saturday morning. The sun hadn't crested over the trees yet, only turned the air gray enough to see fog hanging heavy above the ground. The first cup of coffee tasted like a second one, and Merrill drowsed at my feet as I sat in my favorite chair with the Volks' iPad on my lap.

The device must've been Bethany's—the colors matched her room decor. It was innocuous enough, but the state it was in combined with where I'd found it raised too many questions.

The twentieth or so attempt to turn it on produced the same result as before. It was so much useless junk now. Just a bunch of broken glass and darkened circuits. Nothing to obsess over. And yet . . .

A quick check of Kaylee's channel confirmed what had been drifting in the back of my mind like an eye floater passing in front of a retina. The big goddamn purple teddy bear. I'd seen it before and hadn't realized where until waking up that morning. Bethany could be seen in at least a dozen of Kaylee's posts with the stuffed animal tucked under one arm or clutched tight to her chest. Which raised another question: If it was Bethany's, what was it doing in Andrea's room?

So to summarize, we had a dead family, a possible drug addiction, a child's broken iPad, and a stolen stuffed animal. My finger tapped the iPad's case in a solemn drumbeat. Merrill raised his head and whined.

"You think so? That's a pretty bold assumption. It could just be a kid's iPad—video games and face-changing apps and nothing else." Merrill blinked and lowered his head to the floor, letting out a long sigh. "Yeah, me, too, buddy. Me too."

Scanning the news produced nothing new regarding the Volks. It was still a top story, but no more bodies had been found. Somewhere out there Justin's and Andrea's remains were floating. Maybe they'd wash in, maybe they wouldn't. It might be months or years before they were discovered, caught in some fisherman's net or by a kid stumbling on a set of bones on some remote beach. Without fresh blood the news cycle would eventually move on, people would look to the new headline for their fix, and the Volks would fade into obscurity. Another mystery, its only mystique being it was unsolved.

The coffee tasted bitter, and I emptied the dregs into the sink. After dressing and feeding Merrill I started to leave, attempting to ignore the iPad's presence on the kitchen counter, but it had a gravitational pull all its own and was in my hand as I went out the door.

There are certain spaces—apartments, houses, condos sometimes—reserved near and around courthouses. They're inconspicuous and tax-payer funded. Their use is determined by need. Sometimes there's a witness willing to flip on other criminal personalities who needs safe harbor. Sometimes there are recent parolees unable to live in typical halfway houses who take up residence in them. These spaces are random, undistinguished, and safe for those finding themselves in between circumstances. Julia Roust waited outside one such place now.

She stood with her son beneath an oak tree, both of them wearing backpacks, and a knot inside me uncoiled. I hadn't been sure they would show this morning after leaving her a message the day before, so approaching them on the sidewalk I couldn't help but smile.

"Good morning," I said. Julia nodded a hello. Her bruises were healing, and her ear actually resembled an ear again. "I'm glad you came."

"Almost didn't," Julia said. Sam gave me a look echoing his mother's reply.

"Why don't we go inside, and I'll show you around."

"Hold up a second. What's all this about anyway? You call and leave a weird message to bring a few changes of clothes and meet you here but don't say why."

"The courthouse is right down the block. You need to check in there with an administrator as per your probation. And you work on this side of town, right? The bus ride would be a lot shorter from here." She eyed me with something bordering suspicion but followed when I led the way up the walk.

The ground-floor apartment was spacious, clean, and welcoming without being overdone. There were a few cheap art prints on the walls, and the kitchen was stocked with food and dishes. Two bedrooms sat across the hall from one another with a large bathroom at its end. Sam ran through the rooms, tossing his backpack on one of the beds before climbing up to jump a little bit. Julia scolded him halfheartedly, and he went careening back the way he'd come, exploring. The backyard was fenced and held a kid's pool as well as a sandbox. Trees ringed the rear of the property, and only one other apartment (empty—I'd checked) had access to the area.

Julia's eyes traveled over everything, seeming to catalog and judge. She never said a word, only looked around like she was seeing these common everyday objects for the first time.

When the tour was done and Sam was running a rusted truck through a swale of dirt in the sandbox, Julia turned and said, "Okay, what's the deal?"

"No deal, it's just a place to stay," I said, not looking at her. Sam held my attention—the solemn little boy with the distrustful eyes had been shed like old skin, and here was a bright, new creature with play and discovery pumping through his veins. This was how a kid should be. This was what I'd signed up for.

"Bullshit. There's always a deal."

There were a lot of things I could've told her. I could've told her I'd called in a favor with my friend Sara in placement services who had in turn called in a favor. I could've said there'd been three tedious requisition forms to fill out online. I could've told her since there was no state or county authorization, there was no allotted funding for the apartment even though it was vacant. I could've said I'd transferred two months' rent out of my savings and into a state trust account along with signing an occupation agreement so stipulated it could've stood up on its own.

But I didn't tell her any of that. Instead I said, "You can stay here until we find a new permanent place. Somewhere he won't know to look for you."

She opened her mouth, closed it. Opened it again. "I don't know if I can afford this."

"It's taken care of."

The tangible pride rose in Julia again, straightening her back, squaring her shoulders. "We don't need charity."

"This isn't," I said, finally facing her. "It's a reset. A place to get your bearings again. You told me he'd kill you, right?" After a long pause she nodded. "This is the first step in making sure that never happens."

We stood silent for a while, just watching Sam play. After a time Julia said, "Okay. Okay."

Okay. Okay.

Good enough for me.

17

THIS IS REALLY HARD TO SAY | KAYLEE VOLK

100,267 VIEWS * OCT 15, 2022

Kaylee Volk (Volks At Home)

1.1M SUBSCRIBERS

A PUBLIC STATEMENT Please bear with me during this difficult time.

Video Plays

Kaylee appears onscreen. She still looks terrible, but her eyes hold more clarity than in the last video. Her hair has been washed, and she's sitting at a table instead of in bed.

KAYLEE

Hi, everyone. Thanks for all the well wishes. I've been able to read, not all, but most of your comments, and have to say—I couldn't ask for better supporters. If you've emailed me I appreciate you reaching out, but due to the sheer volume I'm unable to reply to everyone. I know you understand.

Kaylee looks away and licks her swollen lips, wincing slightly. She shifts the camera, then faces the lens again.

KAYLEE

For those asking about my condition, I'm getting better. Stronger every day. The doctors say I might even be able to go home fairly soon, which would be a blessing. But—

(a long pause)

—I'm not sure if I can ever go back to that house. It's so empty now. I'm so empty now.

She tries to continue, but her voice cracks. She fumbles with the camera, and the video cuts.

Video resumes, and Kaylee seems to have regained some composure.

KAYLEE

(smiling painfully)

Sorry, it's not easy. Grief shows up in waves. It's strange how it's gone for a little while, then comes raging back when you don't expect it.

(a pause)

I know there's been a lot of talk and speculation about the accident, and I want to make a statement about what happened. I need to say the truth, even if it hurts.

(she blinks several times)

It wasn't an accident.

There's a moment of silence as the gravity of what she's saying collects.

KAYLEE

I can't go into too many details right now, I wouldn't be able to make it through without breaking down, but the bottom line is this—Andrea Parish, our foster daughter, a deeply damaged young woman who we took into our home . . . betrayed us.

Kaylee struggles, her eyes shimmering with tears.

KAYLEE

For reasons we might never understand, Andrea forced our plane down that day. She was deeply disturbed and not only wanted to end her life, but to end the rest of her family's lives as well.

Tears run down Kaylee's face, and she wipes them away gingerly.

KAYLEE

I've made a statement to the police and will be doing an interview on a major news network soon where I'll be able to go into more detail.
(a brief pause while she wipes away more tears)
I wish I would've seen the warning signs. I wish I could have helped her before it came to this, but now there's nothing . . . nothing I can do but tell what happened.

Kaylee swallows some of her emotion and takes a deep steadying breath.

KAYLEE

I thank God for every one of you out there, for your support and your love. Your messages have given me comfort and courage. I can't tell you how much that means. Thank you.

Video Ends

18

The dockyards have a specific smell.

There's the sea, sure, those universal scents of salt and wet rock and cool air that could've been in Japan the week before. But there's also the smell of old creosoted pilings and seagull shit. There's the smell of grease and oil, of grain or rice spilled when a pallet tips from a forklift. The walloping scent of organic decay.

All of these in a single breath, their stories triggering memories. Memories of being a kid after we'd been freed of the closet and my father was dead and ash along with his victims. Memories of coming to a place like this with my shiny new foster family, Stephen and I trailing behind them like two well-cared-for afterthoughts. Fishing from a pier, and tangy mustard on hot dogs from a vendor cart. A plastic kite in the shape of a pirate ship hanging way out over the sea like a ghost of some real wreck.

As I made my way down the concrete stairs to the docks, these things washed over me. Good memories for the most part, but always tinged with melancholy. Because there was a negative space ever present. A void where someone else should've been.

The main docks were a bustle of activity even on a Saturday. Ships were moored in deeper water, and smaller vessels off-loaded their cargo. Loud men in coveralls and stocking caps called to one another and hauled crates to trucks while half a dozen forklifts whined and threaded their way among piles of pallets.

Evan Baker drove one of the forks. He was easily recognizable from his booking photo even though it was four years old. Prison hadn't aged him the way it did older cons. Besides a koi fish freshly inked on one forearm and having gained at least fifteen pounds of muscle, he looked the same.

I waited near the panel truck he was loading until it was full before waving at him. Evan looked at me, then glanced around, eyeing what could only be his foreman farther down the shore. His boss was in deep conversation with a man in a gray suit. Evan gave me another look, then zipped the fork off to the side as the truck he'd loaded drew away.

"Evan Baker?" I asked.

"Yeah?" he said, stepping out of the machine. He was taller than I expected and even more powerfully built. Up close his time inside betrayed my earlier assessment in the wrinkles around his eyes and mouth. There was also something odd in the way he moved. A limp? No. Something else.

"I'm Nora McTavish with state child services. I was wondering if I could speak to you about your sister?"

He tilted his head back and threw another glance at his boss, who was still occupied. "I'm on the clock."

"I understand. This'll only take a minute."

He sighed, shoving his hands deeply into his pockets. "All right. Go."

"I'm following up on an incident that happened last month with your sister's foster children."

"Don't know anything about that, haven't seen her in years."

Shit. "You've had no contact with her or her family?"

"Nope. Nada. Only heard about what happened on the news. Doesn't seem like there's much to investigate. Crazy bitch they were housing crashed the plane, right?"

That dizzying sensation of stepping off an amusement park ride. "How did you know that?"

"Kaylee said so herself. Put it on that video channel she's got."

My thoughts spun. "I guess I wasn't aware of that."

Evan issued a humorless laugh. "Posted about an hour ago. People put everything on the internet."

I tourniquetted the flow of this new revelation and tried to move on. "So you never met their foster daughter Andrea?"

He crossed his arms. "What's this all about? You some kind of cop?"

"No."

"You sound like one."

"I'm just trying to figure out why this happened."

"People snap. That's it."

"I think it's usually a little deeper than that."

Evan turned and headed toward the forklift. "Take it from me—it ain't," he said over one shoulder.

"So your father just snapped?"

It stopped him cold. He faced me again. "What did you say?" When I didn't respond he advanced on me, his size growing, towering. I stood my ground until we were inches apart. "My father was a fucking coward," he breathed in my face. "A lying, thieving coward who hung his family out to dry. And Kaylee's just like him. She never once came to see me inside. Not once. Not her or Natalie. As far as I'm concerned she's someone else's problem. Now leave me alone. I've got work to do."

As he climbed into the forklift, I threw out a final Hail Mary. "There's rumors Justin was using. Maybe Andrea too."

Evan stared at me, then laughed, this time with gusto. "So that's what this is about. Doesn't matter I did my time and I've been clean for years, right? Hit up the addict." He shook his head, then pointed toward the parking lot. "Exit's that way."

Evan backed the fork up and swung it around in a hard turn, speeding toward a low row of pallets. I followed his final directions when the dock foreman sighted me and started down the planking, coming at a brisk walk. Without a look back I left the sights and smells of the dockyard behind.

19

Stephen's backyard was an oasis.

Behind his tidy bungalow on the top of a hill at the dead end of a small neighborhood was another world. Just as Stephen had pursued a career spectrums distant from the situation we grew up in, his backyard was a rebellious statement—a distraction in its detailed extravagance.

Around the side of his house the backyard was fenced by tall boards. A single entrance normally locked was propped open, and music and voices spilled out. The yard itself was perhaps three car lengths wide and long, the lawn thick and even.

Strings of muted yellow lights draped back and forth so that when you looked up, a ceiling of mellow stars was all you could see.

Four stone tables sat equidistant, with paver bricks running between them while an ever-circulating stream gurgled its way along one edge.

A folding bar stood near the house's back deck, and it was behind the mahogany top that Stephen stood, a drink in one hand, holding court with a dozen or so guests.

"By the time he got to the counter, I realized he'd stripped naked," Stephen was saying. "So here's this guy, so covered in hair it took me a second to realize he wasn't wearing some sort of weird tracksuit."

Stephen's friends laughed, one of them saying, "Oh my God, what did you do?"

"I pretended not to notice and served him a large Americano."

"No!"

"Yes. And I told him it was really hot so be careful not to spill."

The crowd howled and I smiled. I'd heard some iteration of the story a few times, but it was always amusing, especially since it was true. Some of the group returned to the tables to play a drinking game where you had to come up with the most random fact by going around in a circle. The person who told the most outlandish thing that could be proven didn't have to drink a shot while all the others did. The game never lasted very long.

Your fingernails and hair don't keep growing after you die; your skin shrinks so it only looks like they do.

Squirrels cause most power outages.

It's only sixty miles to space. And so on.

Stephen caught my attention and waved me inside the house.

The music in the backyard hushed the moment he shut the door, and Stephen motioned toward the kitchen table. "Sit. I got a new bottle of bourbon, and I'm not sharing it with those heathens out there."

When he placed a half full tumbler on the table and dropped into a seat to my right, I realized he was slightly drunk. "Having fun?" I asked, sipping the bourbon. It was smoothly oaky. Delicious.

"You know, anticipation is always better than reality. But yes, it's fine. I'm glad you came. I didn't know if you'd show."

"I told you I would."

"And you were also really preoccupied. Did you go surfing?"

"I did, actually."

"Good. Did it help?"

My finger traced the glass's rim. "Do you still talk to Leigh?"

Stephen wrinkled his nose. "Why?"

"Curious."

"He stops into the shop once in a while. Makes small talk and casually pokes around to find out if I'm seeing anyone. He thinks he's so much slyer than he is. It's one of the reasons we broke up."

"That and he thought you were into an open relationship."

"That had a bearing as well, yes." Stephen fetched a glass of chardonnay from the fridge and leaned back in his chair, assessing me. "You okay?"

"Yeah. Lots of work, that's all."

"Gah, are you ever going to get out of that job?"

I hesitated. Stephen typically kept deeper opinions to himself. It was only with sufficient libation they were revealed. "I think it's all I know how to do."

"Come on. You could do anything you want."

"I want to pilot a steampunk dirigible with a talking monkey sidekick and twenty gallons of rum."

His eyes crinkled. "Who the hell doesn't?"

We drank. Someone tripped over a planter on the back porch to uproarious laughter. The music's pace dropped, and a few couples slow danced under the lights.

"Nice to know people will give you their time," he mused, watching out the window. "The only thing we really have to give, and it's special. *Time*'s just another word for love."

"You're drunk." I nudged his knee with my foot, and he grinned.

"Tell me what it is."

"What what is?"

He favored me with a slanted look. "What you're carrying. You told me about the boy who died. What else is on your back?"

I'd hoped to be more circuitous, more subtle. We all want to be strong, and being strong is being right. I didn't know if Stephen would agree. My hand found Bethany's iPad in my purse and drew it out, setting it on the table between us.

"And what is that?"

"Something I need help with."

Stephen kept his eyes on the iPad but finished his glass of wine in one long swallow. "Who does it belong to?"

"A girl."

"Is she dead too?" I knew he meant it as a joke, but when I didn't answer he said, "Jesus Christ, Nora."

"All you'd have to do is ask Leigh to get it going. It won't turn on."

"Why?"

"I don't know, that's why I need your help."

"No, smartass, why this? What are you doing?"

I hesitated. Here was the one person in the world I could be honest with, something as precious as time, and I couldn't bring myself to tell him why. Obsession is caustic. It strips all reason away. Stephen watched me wrestle for a moment, then stood up and went to the window. He watched the people in the backyard dance.

"Do you know why I don't talk about him?" Stephen spoke so low it took a moment to understand what he said. What he meant. "Because sometimes I wake up, and I'm still in that place. I can smell it." He turned back to me. "I can smell our shit and piss. I can hear those screws being turned in and out. Any second I think the door will open and that fucking monster will come inside and kill all of us." To my horror tears streamed from beneath his glasses. I stood and went to him, tried to hug him, but he pushed me back gently. "No one asked him to do that. No one asked him to give us his food. Why did he do that?"

He let me hug him then. Soft sobs breathed into my shoulder. We held one another as the party's sounds ebbed and flowed. When he let me go his eyes were red, but his tears had stopped. I got him a paper towel he blew his nose on.

"It's okay," I said.

He laughed shakily. "It's not. You know it's not. Only fools say it's okay." He studied me in the low light. "Do you love me?"

"Of course."

"Then you won't have a problem with me saying no."

I finished my drink. "I wouldn't ask—"

"If it weren't important, I know, I know." He turned away. "I want to help you, but I really don't know what that looks like anymore."

I watched him for another beat, then went to the table to grab the iPad, hesitated, and left it where it was before starting toward the door.

"I think about him." Stephen said, looking at his oasis again. "I just don't wish it had been me like you do."

My reply curdled and came apart in my mouth. I left him standing near the window.

20

Bitter truth is that pill we can't get ourselves to swallow.

It's the medicine we get force-fed by the ones who love us. And even when we know it's good for us, we spit it out the moment they're not looking.

The drive home was a blur of resentment. Doubt rode shotgun.

Merrill greeted me like always at the door, his little jig of delight brightening my mood. A full glass of wine took the baton handed off from Stephen's bourbon, and I went to the basement to stand in front of my corkboard of successes.

Maybe this was enough. These pictures of smiling children, happy families. Maybe grinding and getting a win from time to time was sufficient. Maybe Stephen was right. Because what he was really saying was he didn't want to lose me like he had Paul. My throat tightened. It loosened with more wine.

Outside on the deck the air was cool and still. In the distance the sea hushed. Merrill did a big stretch, and I complimented him on it. He grinned and lay near my feet. My mind wandered.

Andrea had been seeing someone, that was a surety, and Taylor knew who it was. She'd all but confirmed it with her denial. This mystery person was suspect numero uno as to who had been in the Volks' house with me. And what exactly had they been doing there? Trying to remove evidence? That seemed right. What evidence? Drugs? Had the stuffed animal been a stash for pills? Or something else? Possible. But that still didn't answer why Andrea had done what she'd done. Taylor said she was always looking for something else, something better. And judging by her sketches, the girl had talent, dreams, aspirations. Did that seem like someone who was planning on offing herself and her family? On the flip side those attributes could become burdens. How many brilliant people had fallen under the weight of unattainable desires? When you didn't have opportunity, hope could become chains.

A squirrel chattered in a nearby tree, and Merrill raised his head, watching, then relaxed. "So Justin was using," I said quietly. Merrill glanced at me, then closed his eyes. "Which made him unable to stop Andrea from crashing the plane." This was according to Kaylee combined with the empty pill bottle in Justin's trash. But was there another explanation, a more reasonable and rational one? Sure, and it went something like this:

Justin had a secret drug addiction and indulged a little too much prior to the family trip. As he lost control of the plane, Andrea tried to save them. Without proper training or know-how, she lost control, giving Kaylee the impression—during a brief high-duress situation—that she was responsible for the crash. Memories were strange things, malleable at best, and Kaylee could've easily misinterpreted Andrea's helping for harm.

Yes. That was the simplest explanation. Occam's razor cutting cleanly through the bullshit. But it lacked something. Some core ingredient that should've stopped my internal alarm from sounding. Finding the identity of whoever had been in the Volks' house was the key. They'd be able to shed light on Andrea and her secrets. They held the hidden part of the story.

A car's engine started somewhere close, breaking the contemplative stillness. Movement came through the trees near the end of my drive, and for a brief moment Byron was visible behind the wheel of his vehicle as it pulled away.

I remained where I was for a minute, listening to the fading crackle of tires, then went inside and locked the door behind us.

———

Sleep's a funny thing. It's amorphous as steam, seeming to come and go at a whim of its own. It favors some and shuns others. It comes in technicolor dreams and deathlike comas. Sleep is fickle and undeniable.

Between the bourbon and the wine, sleep fell like a hammer, knocking me cold. The kind of rest you don't realize you're partaking in until you surface, bleary-eyed and memory wiped as the day you're born. And the worst is waking and not knowing why.

The ceiling of my bedroom came into focus between blinks. Dark with slats of lighter shadow strained through the window shades. The bed was cool and soft, the phone was not ringing or announcing a text message, my heart beat slow and regular—not quite enough booze to plummet the blood pressure tonight. So what woke me?

It was something. Not a random surfacing to reposition myself, none of that. Sitting up brought Merrill into view. He stood at the bedroom door, facing out into the rest of the house, ears cocked. Listening.

A soft thud came from the front of the house.

My prior plodding heart rate stutter-stepped, then double-timed. Merrill, the most laid-back canine ever, released a subsonic growl. So that was it, a sound woke me. On a list of the worst things to wake to in the dead of night, strange sounds were up there.

Climbing out of bed was an effort, both because sleep was still a solid weight on my body and because it was the last thing I wanted to do. Putting a hand on Merrill's back caused him to flinch, and I whispered quiet assurances.

Faint light from a half moon coated the hallway floor. Merrill followed at a close heel on the way to the kitchen. Every few steps we paused, listening. The big windows on the back of the house let in more light, but they also turned the house into a fishbowl—anyone could look in. And in the wide-open space there were few places to hide. I kept close to the wall, watching for a shadow that didn't belong on the back deck or any furtive movement, all the while attempting to grow eyes in the back of my head. A sudden undeniable fear the front door would be cracked open abated upon seeing it still closed, still locked. The door's glass was frosted, obscuring everything on the other side during the brightest of days. Now there were only dark, vague shapes visible—trees or a serial killer equal possibilities.

All the second-guesses and should'ves rose as they do when hearing irregular noises at night and knowing there'll be no more sleep until you've identified them.

The wanton craving for a security system.

The itchy palm for a gun you don't own.

The cringe of realizing you left your phone at the other end of the house.

Even wishing you'd invited your suffocating boyfriend to stay the night.

Something creaked outside the door.

My stomach leaped back while I stayed in place. Merrill released another low growl. The seconds stretched to minutes. Nothing. Not even the wind. A tree branch then. Or some animal, a raccoon scurrying across the deck, maybe making a mess in one of the flowerpots. It explained Merrill's reaction too. But it wasn't convincing enough to warrant opening the door. No, thank you.

"Come on," I whispered, snagging Merrill's collar. He came easily enough, padding along in silence.

Those night sounds. The clicks and pops—innocuous 99.9 percent of the time—caused a disproportionate amount of panic. They stirred something in our lizard brains dating back to when we feared the night and what it brought to our cave doors. Now they were plastic bags uncrinkling beneath the sink or the pressure in a pipe equalizing. Even a little mammal traipsing across our porch.

Something passed by the kitchen window.

My hand flew to my mouth, stifling a reactionary yell. Merrill passed by, completely unaware as the shape dislodged from a clump of shadows next to the house and moved out of sight down the hill.

Upright. Big. Not a raccoon at all.

None of this is happening.

My legs were flaccid, the bones dissolved. The need to both see who was out there as well as run and hide drew and quartered me. Paralyzed me on the spot. Merrill glanced back once as if to say, *What's the problem, human? Thought you said we were good?*

Someone was outside the house. They'd been on the front porch poking around, and now they were circling down to the walkout side where the ground dropped away. Down to the basement with all the sliding windows and door—

Was the basement door locked?

My stomach was again on the move without me, racing ahead toward the stairs and down them, then across the basement to the door and holy shit why would I remember locking it when I rarely used it? It could be open. It shouldn't be, but it could be.

Except I hadn't moved. Not an inch. My phone. Had to get the phone, then down to see if the basement door was locked. Without a phone there would be no way to call for help.

The floor wobbled beneath me, a surge of adrenaline mainlining through my veins hard enough to create bursts of light at the corners of my vision. My phone was on the bedroom table and was at a walloping 3 percent charge because of course it was. Merrill started to lie down at the foot of the bed but hopped up again when I exited the room at a half run.

Opening the phone and punching in nine-one-one going downstairs at the same time was a mistake. My foot turned on the second to the last tread, and then the wall at the bottom of the stairs was coming up too fast. My shoulder and the side of my head met drywall with a solid thunk, and I barely maintained balance enough to stay upright. Staggering around the corner into the main basement space, I cupped the phone screen to shield it from anyone looking in from outside. The emergency number was queued up and ready to go, ready to zip out a distress beacon the moment my finger touched the send key.

At a glance there was nothing of note outside the windows, no shapes or shadowy movement. Nothing alarming. Just the yard sloping away to the surrounding trees and brush. Still navigating in the dark, we moved forward, Merrill pacing me with his head low to the carpet.

The basement door stood ahead, still closed. Good so far. As we neared, my swimming night vision gradually sought out the dead bolt and its position. Locked. I time traveled and quickly high-fived my former self for her sense of responsibility. As I sidled up to the door my fingers touched the two locks, double-checking their solidity before leaning to the left to peer out the nearest window.

The moon transformed the backyard into a deepwater aquarium.

Ambient light shimmered, causing everything to move and ripple.

Panning from one side of the space to the other brought nothing of interest into focus. Nothing moved. A long breath came out of me in a quiet rush, and I placed one forearm against the cool wood of the door, leaning my forehead against my arm. Even as I did so an image solidified of someone in almost the exact same position on the opposite side of the door, our bodies inches apart.

I shifted to the right enough to look out the other window. No one was outside the basement door. No one was on the lawn. Nothing moved in the density of the trees. Whoever it had been was gone. A drunk maybe. Someone stumbling through the neighborhood trying to take a shortcut. The explanation acted like an analgesic to the alarm. No one was trying to get into the house. Why would they be?

To rape and kill you, dumbass. Yes, the old standby fear and ever-present threat all women seemed to harbor—its merits proven valid over and over again on the evening news. But this time it had been some rando meandering across the property at night, probably not a single ill intention in his body.

As I started to turn away from the window, something caught my eye. A deeper shadow beside a bush at the corner of the yard. Hunched and more solid than its surroundings. I squinted, breathing shallow.

The shape had a person-like essence. Part of a head and shoulder. A hip. My hand tightened on my phone. Was it watching me? Could it see me?

None of this is happening.

Something soft and wet touched the back of my knee.

A strangled shriek climbed up my throat, and I sagged to the side, glancing down in horror even as my mind explained what had happened. Merrill had licked my leg. He panted, looking up at me with questioning eyes. I cursed under my breath and looked out the window again.

The shadow was gone.

21

Just like the night strips away reason and common sense, leaving us with unmitigated fears of what could be lurking beyond the firelight, the day fills us with an overconfidence bordering on stupidity.

When the first rays of sun cut between the trees, it was enough to convince me there hadn't really been anyone standing in the corner of my yard watching the house. It had been the middle of the night. I'd still been bleary with sleep. Yes, there'd been someone outside, a person trespassing on my property, but had they hidden at the edge of view, watching and waiting like some kind of predator? No. Probably not.

Outside, the dew was unbroken, the lawn a silver carpet. There were no footprints sullying it. Not that it really proved anything; I had no idea when the dew point was.

My coffee steamed as I followed the route the figure had seemed to take, Merrill loping along the outer edge of the property searching for a place to do his morning business. There were no visible signs of passage or disturbance, but my experience with tracking people through the wild was limited to television and certain western novels.

An inspection of the basement door revealed no clues, just as a sweep of the front porch had yielded nothing. Perhaps Byron could bring a fingerprint kit out and dust both doorknobs. That particular notion lingered for all of two seconds before it was dismissed.

At the corner of the yard where the shadow had appeared to watch me, I faltered. It wasn't fully light back here, the shade like tide pools beneath the trees. Merrill had wandered away toward the front of the house, and I was alone. At least it appeared so.

There was a flattened area beside the bush, as if someone had stood there for a time recently. Or maybe it was just how the ground always looked. A quick search of the surrounding area revealed nothing else, no suggestions of human presence, no hair or fibers on any of the brush, yet my skin crawled.

I looked around the semidark woods. At this hour on a Sunday morning there were no usual sounds of hustle or bustle in the neighborhood. Most were asleep and hadn't yet started the day's activities. If someone came bursting out from the underbrush now, would anyone hear me scream?

Listening past the sound of my heartbeat, there was no chirring of crickets or birds calling to one another, no squirrel chatter. The woods were quiet. Still.

All at once the need to be away from the hanging shadows and unnatural silence was overpowering. I backed away from the woods a good ten steps. Enough for a head start if someone began chasing me up the slope. And even though no one appeared from behind any trees or brush, halfway to the front door I broke into a run.

———

The day of rest stretched out cloudy and cool with spates of rain. After securing a light breakfast and the day's supplies, we departed the house. I needed a little time away since even its bright, open spaces felt cloistering. I double-checked all the locks before we left.

We waited out a longer cloudburst in a café's covered patio, the rain metronoming on the canvas roof. More coffee and a treat for Merrill.

Then we were leaving the city for the foothills, muddled and dark on the near horizon.

We ended up on a tributary of a trail named Eagle View. It broke off from the main path a mile from the trailhead and jagged up a rock face through trees that had been old when Europeans were nosing their boats to shore on the opposite coast.

Merrill kept pace with me as the last of the other weekend hikers fell away behind us. Few knew about this place, and fewer still traversed it. Most stayed to the well-tended trails, the picturesque lookouts over streams and waterfalls where they could snap selfies or brag on social media. We ran when we could, slowed to a near vertical crawl when we couldn't. In the early afternoon it rained, soaking us. The fear of the night before began sloughing away like stubborn grime.

The last of the hike brought us to the top of a mountain. I didn't know its name, didn't want to. There is a freedom in anonymity. Liberty in losing yourself in a place that's yet to be exploited. It purifies, even if we don't deserve it.

We stopped under a rock outcropping to take in the view. Swaths of old-growth trees spread out below the drop, and a river raged through a canyon, soundless two miles distant. As much as I loved the ocean, loved surfing, this place without its pollution of noise and people living their lives was better.

A wheel turned in my head. Here was Stephen outlined at his backyard window, his tears soaking into the fabric of my shirt. Here was Mason Roberts, quiet and resolute—already looking forward to a life of promise that wouldn't come. Bethany Jacobs sang her songs and held her purple bear. Andrea Parish drew her eloquent designs and dreamed of never running away again.

And Paul. Paul smiled and closed his eyes.

The trick is finding a place so quiet, so full of solitude, you don't have to think over the din—the noise other minds create. Your own creates enough by itself. Everyone should have a place to retreat to, somewhere unique that doesn't belong to anyone, not even you. When there are no distractions, you can get down to business. Let the terrible things out of their cages you keep inside. Face them as fully as you can, let them hurt you. Bones are the strongest at a break site while they're mending. Scar tissue is fibrous so it's tougher than skin.

We're told a life without pain is ideal. To avoid suffering as much as possible. But pain is where you grow. We cry with our first breaths because it hurts to expel amniotic fluid and take in air. No transition occurs without pain. It's why liminal spaces are uniform and ambiguous—to lull before the change. Before the pain.

Sitting on a stone beneath the rock outcropping that would remain for a thousand years after my death, I cried. I cried for the things that were gone and for what would come. I let it in. I let it break me.

When it was over the rain had moved on, sweeping away across the valley behind the clouds it fell from. Merrill laid his head on my feet and looked up at me. My eyes were dry. It was time to go.

———

By the time we arrived home it was bordering dark, the sky remained overcast, and the ocean was smeared bloody in the west. But there was enough light to see something was wrong. I sat in the car staring at the house, swimming in a mire of shock.

Then I picked up my phone to dial Byron, all the while taking in the shattered wood of the doorjamb and how my front door itself hung askew like a broken jaw.

22

Those people on TV you see with the hollow stares, the bombed-out eyes.

The ones who have survived something and know a new truth. A hurricane has swept their daughter away, or a fire has burned all their possessions. Their vulnerable father is missing, or their store has been robbed. They've been violated in some way, and people watch from their living rooms shaking their heads, glad they don't understand.

I knew I looked like them. Had always belonged to that particular group of refugees moving onward from some smoking tragedy in their past. But it becomes inured in your life—another aspect of who you are. People can get used to anything given enough time. You make as much peace as you can and try to go forward.

Now I wondered if that same look had resurfaced on my face and made an effort to submerge it again, to nod in the right places as the officer explained the house was clear and there'd be a patrol in the neighborhood for the next few nights. No, I didn't think anything was missing. Yes, I'd call if I found something was.

Then the flurry of activity over the last two hours wound down until everyone was gone except Byron.

He'd stood in the background for the most part. This after I'd rebuffed his embrace upon his arrival. I didn't need hugs, I needed to know if someone was still in my goddamned house. Now he busied himself double-checking the repairs on the front door a security agency had seen to. I'd poured myself a whiskey I couldn't get myself to drink and stood in the kitchen, taking in the wreckage of my home.

Whoever had forced the door knew I wasn't home. They'd been patiently watching, waiting to see when I left—most likely since the night before after casing the place. Now the crawling sensation of eyes on my skin that morning made more sense. I broke out in goose bumps for a third time.

They'd gone like a whirlwind through the house, starting in the entry and working their way inward. Books pulled off shelves, cupboards emptied. Glass shone in sprays on the floor, and the dressers in my bedroom had been gutted. The entire place looked like it had been hit by a personalized earthquake. One made just for me. This violation of my private space. And it shook me to see the things that made up my life scattered without care.

Because I knew what they'd been looking for.

"Door should be good. At least for now," Byron said, coming into the kitchen. He knelt and petted Merrill where he lay at my feet. "I know a carpenter over on Fifth who does good work. He remodeled my mom's kitchen. I can have him come by and do an estimate."

"Thanks. Leave me his number," I said.

Byron patted Merrill a last time and stood, hands shucked into his pockets. For a second he just looked at me. "You okay?"

"Yeah. It's just a shock to come home to this."

He glanced around. "You're sure you didn't see anything last night? Nothing identifying about whoever was outside? No suspicious cars or people?"

"Other than you parked out front?" The words were out before I could stop myself.

He sighed, still watching me. "I came by to talk."

"Why didn't you call?"

"Because I was in the area. And half the time you don't answer." I waited. "So that's a no?"

"No, like I said, I couldn't see who it was. A guy or a large woman, I don't know."

"I'll do some checking, see if there's been any other break-ins in the area. Maybe this fits a pattern." I took a small swig of my drink, waiting for what I knew was coming. "Want me to stay over?" he asked after a beat.

"No, I'm good."

He pushed his hands even deeper into his pockets, looking at a spot on the wall for a time before facing me again. "So what's it gonna be?" he said finally.

"What's what gonna be?"

"This. Us. You let me come over, we fuck, you kick me out. You call when you need something—"

"I've never kicked you out, and I'm not sure it's really a great time for this discussion." I took another slug of whiskey and moved past him, threading through debris toward the basement stairs. Byron followed.

The basement's disarray mirrored the main floor. The couch before the TV was torn apart, cushions scattered. My desk had been autopsied, its contents strewn in a swath of office carnage. And my success board had even been yanked from the wall, pictures of kids staring up from a dozen places on the carpet. I stood the corkboard up and started gathering the printed photos. It hurt to see this more than anything—the small triumphs of my work life tossed and treaded on like they didn't actually matter was a little too on the nose.

"I just want to know where we stand," Byron said quietly.

"I don't know what you want from me," I said, continuing to stack pictures in a little pile on the desk.

"Ditto. I mean, we have a good time together, right? We get along."

I sat back on my haunches. "We do."

"But you won't let me in."

"You're in. You're standing in my basement."

"You know what I mean."

I went back to organizing. Something was wrong—among the sea of wrongness spread around me, something else was amiss. It took a few seconds to realize what it was.

Paul's Saint Anthony medal was gone.

I combed the floor with my hands, crawling first one way, then another, trying to quell the rising panic. It was here. It had to be here somewhere. The irony of looking for a missing Saint Anthony medal wasn't lost on me.

"I try to be supportive and still give you your space. I listen and don't push, but you still give me the brush-off," he continued.

I moved sideways, peering under my desk, running my fingers through the carpet, waiting to feel the cool links of chain. Hoping.

"I mean we've never talked about being exclusive, but I always have been."

Where was it? Why the hell would someone take Paul's medal? Out of spite? Did they know what it meant to me? My hands shook as I turned the opposite way and hunted back toward the couch, the search balancing on the edge of frantic.

"All I want to do is be with you, to help you."

I whirled on him. "See that's just it, you're pushing your help on me." Byron flinched as if he'd been struck. In a way, he had. A part of me tried to wall off the things spilling through the barrier I'd constructed. The part that knew Byron was a good man. As good as I'd probably ever find. He was considerate, caring, kind, comforting, strong, sensitive—all the things to look for in a partner, and all the things he was telling me he was. Which is what demolished the rest of the barrier, and everything came flooding through.

Rising to my feet I said, "I don't need you doing my dishes or stopping by unannounced. I don't want to be checked up on or brought dinner without asking. I don't want any of that."

"Then what do you want?" He held out his hands, palms up. "I get you're independent and—"

"No, you don't get that. Otherwise you'd have figured out what not to do by now."

"I'm not a mind reader. If you don't talk to me, how am I supposed to know what you want?"

"If I'm not talking to you, it means I don't want to talk. It doesn't mean I don't like you." I took a breath. "Look, you're great, and I enjoy spending time with you, but trying to insert yourself fully into my life is not going to work."

He shook his head. "I thought that's what couples did. They shared their lives."

"Maybe some, sure. But that's not who I am. It just isn't."

He was quiet for a second, taking in the surrounding mess. "I know what happened to you when you were a kid really formed you."

"Don't . . ."

"Your father . . . and losing your brother like that, I get it. And I understand why you won't allow yourself to get close to anyone. You're afraid of losing them too."

"So this is where you tell me how you know me better than I know myself?" The volume of my voice climbed. That rational part of me was still trying to do damage control, but it was futile. The missiles were armed. Go for launch. "Yes, please, Byron, explain some insightful truth about me I didn't realize until you said it, and I'll start crying, and you can comfort me." I laughed coldly. "You think I'm still at the stage of being afraid of losing people I care about? I passed that light-years ago. You think I don't understand my own trauma?"

"I didn't say that—"

"I've gone through denial, grieving, self-loathing, you name it. I've lived inside guilt for years. I still do, but I'm not special. Other people have gone through much worse, and I know that. But don't stand there and tell me you understand some intrinsic part of myself I'm unaware of, because you don't. You can't even figure out when I want to be left alone."

"You almost always want to be left alone."

"Then that's me!" I held my arms out wide. "That's who I am. Who I'm not is someone needing to be cooked and cleaned for. I don't need taking care of. It's suffocating. You're forcing your idea of love on me."

He studied me for a long moment, then looked down, nodding. "I guess I am. That's how I show affection. I try to take care of people. That's who *I* am."

My temper fell with the resignation in his voice. "And I'm not asking you to change," I said quietly. "I'm saying if you can't be with me without asking the same, then it's not going to work. Maybe someday it'll be different. Maybe there's a middle ground for us, but for now this is what I have to offer. This is the best I can do."

He nodded again, glancing at me before looking away. He turned and took a couple of steps toward the stairs, then paused. "What were you doing at the Volks' house the other day?"

Whiplash. A pure one-eighty, leaving me stunned. "What day?" was my stupid attempt at a reply.

"Tom Nelson told me you were there the day after the crash. What were you doing?"

The bogus story I'd given Tom wasn't going to work on Byron. I knew it. After a long spate of silence, he knew it too. I stayed quiet.

Byron chewed his lower lip for a moment. Under ordinary circumstances it would've been cute, an endearing tic that would've made me want to kiss him. Now it was hard to watch. "I do care about you. A lot," he said. "That's why I probably should stay away. I don't want to see you hurt yourself. Not anymore."

Then he was leaving the room and treading up the stairs. The front door opened and closed. He was gone.

"Fuck." I turned on my heel and paced a few steps. It was dark now, the night outside turning the basement windows into mirrors where my gauzy reflection floated. Merrill chuffed once, and I went to him, smoothing his ears back. "We're okay. Yeah. We're okay, aren't we?" Merrill seemed to understand it was a rhetorical question and rolled to his side, exposing his belly. I scratched it.

The iPad. That's what they were looking for. I'd known it a few minutes after coming inside and seeing the state of the house. They'd torn everything apart for a child's tablet. For what was on it.

A warning bell tolled once, deep in the recesses of my mind. Then it was quiet. Because I'd already made my choice. I'd already paddled in and was standing up, the wave gathering speed and height behind me. There was no choice but to ride it now.

Something glittered beneath the couch. I stretched out and snagged it, pulling it into the light. My heart sighed. Paul's medal. I wrapped it in my hand and closed my eyes.

23

"Nora, can I see you in my office?"

The last thing you want to hear on a Monday morning. By the time I looked over my shoulder, Kelly had moved past my cubicle, disappearing toward his glassed-in walls. I'd just sat down. My coffee was still hot, but I hadn't drunk enough to fully wake up yet. The path to Kelly's office was a haze, the previous sleepless night trailing behind me like some kind of lethargic comet's tail.

It had taken nearly three hours and four whiskies to clean up the house. Amid the sweeping, scooping, carrying, and replacing, Merrill followed me, staying out of the way while lending his comforting presence. The only solace in the whole mess was having taken him with me on the hike. Otherwise he would've been there whenever the intruder had broken in. I wouldn't think about what could've happened if that scenario played out in another time line.

Could I say I hadn't checked all the windows and doors more than once before going to bed? No. Could anyone blame me? Around two in the morning, while I was still lying awake in a semidrunken fog listening to every tick and click the house made, I began wishing I'd let Byron stay. It was the weak and frightened part of me wanting someone else near even if it were for the wrong reasons. But I respected him too much to use him. Instead I settled for a few straight-backed chairs slid tight under all the doorknobs. The rest of the night before my alarm went off was a dunk tank of dreams, dropping into and out of consciousness until it was difficult to tell if I was awake or not.

Given all that, my tolerance for Kelly's bullshit was near zero. I was on the verge of saying this up front when I entered his office and saw the look on his face.

"Shut the door behind you," he said. There was none of the usual paperwork on his desk, only his hands, fingers intertwined. It seemed I was the only thing on his schedule this morning. I did as he asked. "Sit."

"I'm good," I said after a long moment.

Kelly huffed a short laugh. "You're quite the contrarian, you know that?"

"Sticks and stones . . ."

"I was hoping after our talk last week some of it would've registered to you. But it obviously didn't."

"If this is about Julia Roust, I looked up all the requirements and statutes. I'm well within—"

"It's not," Kelly said, finally laying his clasped hands flat on his empty desk. "I received an email over the weekend from an Evan Baker."

Shit.

"It was followed up by an email from Evan Baker's dock foreman. Do you want to hazard a guess as to what their concerns were about?"

A long breath trailed from me. "Yes, I spoke to him about his sister."

Kelly was shaking his head. "Nora, what are you doing? The Volk case is closed. Whatever happened in its aftermath is none of our concern."

"Maybe it's not yours," I said, keeping as much emotion out of my voice as possible. He wasn't the one out there every day, seeing these kids. Seeing what they went through partially because of our decisions. "You don't see the fallout."

"It's the job!" Kelly said, leaning back in his chair. "You know this better than anyone."

"I was just talking to him. I left when asked."

"Regardless, he and his boss have filed a formal complaint."

Shit. "Okay. What's that mean?"

"It means it'll be passed on to the state board of directors." Kelly let the quiet spool out for a second before dropping the second shoe. "And until they review the complaint and set a meeting date, you're on administrative leave."

"You're kidding."

"What did you think was going to happen? Evan Baker was deeply upset by your questioning. He threatened to get a restraining order unless action was taken. You can't just show up at people's workplaces and badger them about their families."

"I didn't badger him."

"His words, not mine. Again, that's moot." His expression softened. "You're a forensic social worker, and a damned good one too. But you're not a detective. You had no cause to talk to him." He shook his head again and made some paperwork appear on his desktop. "Grab anything you need from your cubicle and go. You'll be informed via email when the state board meets." Kelly began leafing through pages.

I started to reply, then thought better of it. What was the point? Kelly was a single cog in a much greater machine. A machine designed to run on the smallest budget while asking the most of its components. Even if I could convince Kelly there was something bigger going on with the Volks, it wouldn't make an iota of difference. He was right, it wasn't child protective services' concern. So many people's interests stopped at a time clock or paycheck.

We're all to blame.

There was nothing I needed other than my purse in the cubicle. I gave it a quick once over and headed out, and found Richard Jackson blocking my way.

"Nora, Nora, Nora—just the gal I wanted to see." Jackson flashed a smile and tapped a folder on one palm. "Say, you wouldn't be able to help a guy out, would you? I've got a deposition this afternoon and—"

"Pick up your own fucking slack, Rich," I said without slowing down. A couple of heads turned in cubicles, and then I was out the door.

24

Sara Wilson appeared in the restaurant's doorway just as I was starting to think she wouldn't show.

She spotted me where I was sitting at the back near the windows. The view outside was a good one: rocky cliffs, crashing ocean waves, seagulls gliding on updrafts. I'd been taking it all in for a couple of hours along with several tequila sunrises, biding my time until it was late enough to ask Sara to an impromptu brunch.

Sara dropped into the seat across from me, tossing her purse down. The scar from her cleft lip was a thin silver line below her nose. In the morose and sometimes apathetic realm of child services, Sara was a fighter. She cared, and it showed. She was only five years my senior but looked ten, mostly blonde but graying around the edges and harried. Whenever I saw her, I knew I was looking at myself in a few years if I stayed in my position. That was if the state board allowed it.

"Brunch on a Monday morning. This is a first," she said, settling herself, then freezing for a second, seeing my choice of drink. "You take a personal day?"

"You could say that." I motioned for the server to bring another tequila. She waited, not saying anything. Sara was one of those people who never assumed, never overstepped or telescoped her opinions. She was a watcher and listener, wicked intelligent with zero patience for bullshit. I loved her so much.

When there was a fresh glass in front of me, I raised it. "A toast. To the newest member of the prestigious administrative-leave club. I'd like to thank the academy." I drank.

Sara blinked. "Tell me."

I did.

I held nothing back, not even my less-than-legal entering of the Volks' home and what I'd found there. When I was finished she motioned the waiter over. "A vodka tonic on the rocks."

When he'd gone I said, "*Oooo*, drinking on the job. Be careful or you'll be joining me."

"You fucked up," Sara said, voice flat.

"You sound like Kelly."

"He's not wrong."

"I kinda thought you'd—"

"No, no, I'm with you. I can't say I would've done anything different. It's just now you've attracted the attention of someone dangerous."

"Yeah, I added that much up myself."

Sara's drink arrived, and she quickly drank half of it, giving the barest of glances around. The restaurant was mostly empty this time of day. "So they want the tablet or what's on it, but it's broken at the moment."

"Right."

"They must've followed you home. Or overheard you talking to Tom when you showed up and found out who you were."

It hadn't occurred to me that the intruder had already been in the house when I'd arrived. The idea upped the creep factor substantially. "Maybe. In any case, they must've figured I took the iPad and came looking for it. The first night they were casing the place. Then they waited until I left to break in."

"And the teddy bear . . ."

"Yeah." The damned stuffed animal. The fly in the ointment. There was some connection to the iPad, but what, I couldn't say. Just a simmering sense I was overlooking some crucial detail. "The only thing I can think is it was a cash or drug stash. Maybe Justin used it to transfer his stuff in plain sight."

"Kinda weird, though, right?" Sara leaned back in her seat and sipped her drink. "A grown man walking around with a teddy bear might draw more attention than not."

"True. In his own house, though, maybe not so much."

She was quiet for a beat, that steady contemplation I knew so well going on behind her eyes. "So if you get the tablet working again, you'll know who wanted it so bad."

"Hopefully."

"What're you gonna do with your newly acquired vacation time?"

I went to finish my drink, but it was already gone. I stared into its emptiness. "Reason says go home and wait out my suspension. Clean the house. Take up knitting."

"Smart. Safe. What're you actually gonna do?"

I sighed. "Probably something less reasonable."

———

The billboard towered over the building across the street, throwing a long shadow from the sun, which had decided to make a short appearance. I looked at the billboard's advertisement from my car and tilted the seat back, not sure I was good to drive yet. I turned the radio on and drank from a bottle of water. Some poppy auto-tuned cardboard flowed from the speakers. I flipped the channel.

What to do? There were options. Go home and reevaluate my life was one of them. Take into consideration everything that had happened in the last week and reassess. Maybe there was one more person I could alienate in my life. Or maybe it was time to update my résumé. A country singer moaned about his truck and his girlfriend in the same breath, and my fingers twitched at the radio.

The day before, after realizing why someone had ransacked my home, I'd been nearly paralyzed by the fear they would then go to Stephen's and pay him a visit. This notion quickly evaporated because there was no valid reason he would have the iPad in the first place, that being of course if the breaker and enterer even knew of his existence. No, Stephen should be safe, though the urge to call him and double-check was almost overpowering. But if I did that now he would take it as an insinuation about me leaving the device with him and might cause another flare-up between us. I didn't want that for a dozen reasons. A melancholy boy with an English accent and a piano went on and on about how she was gone. I flicked the radio off.

On the billboard a delighted couple sat across a mahogany table from a smiling man in an expensive suit. They were all looking at some papers on the table like they were visas to heaven. Script lined the base of the billboard in bold letters. DON'T TRUST JUST ANYONE WITH YOUR FINANCIAL FUTURE, INVEST WITH THE BEST AT VOLK INVESTMENTS.

The sun slid behind a bank of clouds, and I put the car in gear.

25

Volk Investments took up one floor of the tallest high-rise in downtown.

The building itself, already phallically compensating, attempted further intimidation with its mystery-tinted windows allowing zero view of what its interior might hold.

When I stepped off the elevator, a receptionist held me at bay and gave me a hard look when I told her I'd like to speak with Mr. Volk. No, I didn't have an appointment. When I showed her my ID and said it had to do with his son and daughter-in-law, I felt the point of no return appear, then zip past as she spoke low into her headset before sending me through a set of glass doors.

Augustus Volk's private office sprawled in ugly tan carpets and woodwork while floor-to-ceiling windows overlooked the city. As his personal assistant showed me inside, I took in the views, the compact bar lined with heavy cut-crystal glassware, the neo-modern desk and chairs. A painting at least ten feet long on the nearest wall depicted a raging gray sea, a multimast ship plunging over the largest of swells. Before I could intuit its symbolic connection to financial advisement, the door opened, and Augustus Volk stepped inside.

He must've been nearing sixty but could've easily passed for fifty with the lack of wrinkles, save for around his eyes, and the trim physique beneath his suit. His platinum hair curled to the side in a wave the picture on the wall would've been envious of.

"Miss McTavish, is it?" he said, stepping around the desk to greet me. "Or did my secretary misinform me?" He glanced at my ring finger before shaking my hand.

"Nora is fine," I said. "I'm very sorry for your loss."

He seemed to ignore the latter remark. "Please sit." I settled into the nearest chair while he moved to the bar. "Anything to drink?"

"No, thank you."

"Hope you don't mind," he said, pouring three fingers of amber liquid into a glass. "The last week has been quite devastating. I don't know how many people have told me I shouldn't be here at work. And I'm wondering, where would they have me be then? At home alone? Listless?" He tilted his head as if expecting a reply, and I realized the drink he held wasn't the first, or maybe even the third, of the day. "I think it's less empathy and more that they don't want to bear witness to grief. But I built this company from the ground up. Hired each and every person who's out on that floor, and I'll be damned if they dictate what I do or how I do it," he said, folding himself into the seat behind his desk. He sipped deeply before focusing on me. "So you're with the state then."

"I am. Child services."

"And what can I do for you?"

"I'm looking into an incident that happened a while back with Justin and Kaylee's foster children. Mason and Andrea?"

A sneer crawled across his mouth. "Tell me you're building a civil case."

"I'm sorry?"

"Against that girl's real family. She had to have relatives; they all come from somewhere, right? I'll sign on in a heartbeat if the state's going to trial."

"I'm not aware of any civil suit at this time. I'm trying to piece some things together and figure out if the prior incident had anything to do with last week's tragedy."

Augustus turned slightly in his chair and took another drink. "Tragedy. Funny how words don't always have the same meaning, isn't it? I didn't think of my son when I heard that word before, but now I always will." He sat motionless for a beat before looking at me through a glaze of booze. "She was crazy. That's all I know. Justin told me about her hurting the boy. If I would've known she was capable of this, I would've given her the same treatment and choked the life out of her myself."

I rearranged myself in the chair. This was going downhill fast. "Did Justin say anything else to you before . . . before last week? Anything odd or out of character?"

"No. Nothing. He was always a good boy. Strong and solid. Able to make the hard decisions like I taught him. Finance is a ruthless business, but he had what it took. He wasn't just going to get handed the reins, and he knew it. More than one business was brought low because of sentimental nepotism." He took another drink. "I've always believed we don't owe our children anything. We gave them life, and it's their responsibility to do something with it. They grow up strong that way, responsible. Justin understood that. He was a worker. I wasn't happy about him getting his pilot's license and buying that plane, but it was his money. Do you have children?"

"No."

"Not married then?"

"Were you ever aware of Justin using any kind of drugs?"

It took a moment for him to register what I'd said. "What? No, absolutely not. Why would you ask such a thing?"

"It's a routine question. How about Kaylee?"

"No. She saw what drugs and drink did to her mother. Never knew her to have more than a single glass of wine. Speaking of, you sure you wouldn't like a snifter?" He rose and went to the bar.

"I'm fine, thanks. Do you get along with your daughter-in-law?"

Augustus sloshed his glass full and coughed what might've been a laugh. "Yeah, we get along fine. I just had to hear about her from time to time when that nonsense she does on the internet got to be too much for Justin."

"He didn't approve of her career?"

Augustus let out a full laugh this time. It was cold and hard to listen to. "*Career*. She glossed herself up and grinned into a camera. She was a walking, talking commercial. Justin hated all that nonsense, hated their lives being on display." He started back toward his chair but detoured and instead perched on the edge of his desk, his leg resting a few inches from mine. I shifted away. "Want to know something else?" He leaned in. "He hated those kids too."

All systems red. Full stop. My skin prickled. "He hated their foster children?"

"They weren't his children. Justin wanted kids of his own, not someone else's. But she couldn't give him any, so he went along with her idea. She had to have her perfect family. Instead they got other people's liabilities. I mean, you're a bright young woman, you must know that as well as I do. Good people try to take on these kids, and what do they get for it? Hardship and heartache." His smile was meant to be conspiratorial and charming, but it was haunted with pain and his ugly attempts at engaging me to blunt that pain.

"So you'd say Justin and Kaylee were having problems?" I asked.

"I'd say they would've been better off without those kids. I told him as much not too long ago." He snapped back an alarming amount of his drink and set it down.

"Have you spoken to Kaylee?"

"Once. On the phone." His gaze rested on my thighs and slowly climbed upward.

"And did she say anything else about what happened?"

"I'll tell you what," Augustus said. He leaned forward again, the pungency of bourbon coming off him in waves. "Everyone's been saying

I shouldn't be alone right now, so how about we continue this conversation over lunch? There's a great French restaurant down the street. My treat."

How many young women had sat here in this same exact position? I could almost feel their vestigial presence, their lingering discomfort, radiating around me. That tuning-fork hum of unease and pressure. Pressure to kindly digress, to not make a scene, and get the fuck out of here as quickly as humanly possible.

"Humor a grieving man. What do you say?" He slid the toe of his shoe against my foot.

I stood. "Actually I have all I need." I made my way to the door and stopped, resisted the impulse to be out of his lurid gaze. It felt too much like a retreat. "And for the record," I said, facing him again, "I'm sure you weren't insinuating trading information in an ongoing state child services case on the condition of romantic favors, were you, Mr. Volk? Because otherwise I would have to add that notation to the file. Which would eventually become public information."

A spark of something shone within his alcohol glaze. Indignation. "If you need anything further, you can speak to my lawyer."

"Ah, your lawyer. I'm sure he's very good—*well versed*—in defending you. Have a great day."

I'd have to check the security cameras, but I didn't think my feet touched the floor as I left the building.

———

The wind had come up and tugged at my coat on the way to the car, spitting some rain as well. My phone was buzzing, but I waited until the door was shut to the weather before taking it from my pocket. Instead of Byron's number on the screen, which I'd expected, it was unfamiliar. Muted. Let them leave a message if it was important. I was sure my car's auto warranty was going to expire soon . . .

The exuberance at rebuffing Augustus Volk began to fade, and an ill feeling took its place. For a moment I labeled it as the typical reaction to any icky encounter with the opposite sex, but it was something else.

He hated those kids.

Justin. The good-looking rich boy with the trophy wife and perfect suburban life, hated his foster children. This coming from his own father, someone he'd confided in. Someone who had also told him he'd be better off without them.

The vehicle's air was still. Pure motionless quiet. Soundless rain fell on the windshield, blotting out the surroundings, turning everything outside to a painting smeared with turpentine. What was I thinking? That Justin had caused the crash? That he'd planned the whole thing to somehow rid himself of the responsibilities that had weighed down his life? But if he had, why would he kill Kaylee, as well, not to mention himself? There were so many other ways to reverse the situation he'd found himself in; why choose murder and potentially suicide?

My phone chimed a voice mail. I very nearly disregarded it but wondered if it might be Kelly calling me back to work. A long shot, but I'd take it. Instead Julia Roust's panicked voice met my ear.

"Nora, please, call me back. You have to help. He found us. He must've followed me from work. I saw Frank's car drive by when I got to the apartment."

My stomach became a sack of lead.

"He knows where we are. He's gonna kill me."

26

"What does that mean, there's nothing they can do?"

Julia shifted from foot to foot in the apartment's kitchen, fingers folding and refolding a paper napkin, eyes holding on something for a second before shifting away. The police officers had just exited, their final palaver being with me on the steps outside the apartment. I relayed their parting sentiments.

"Since there's no way to prove it was Frank who drove by—"

"It was him," Julia interrupted. "I'd know that fucking piece-of-shit El Camino anywhere."

The afternoon had drained in waiting. Waiting for the cops to arrive, for them to take Julia's statement about her ex-boyfriend following her from work. Waiting for them to locate and interview him. Then waiting for the officers to return and inform us Julia's ex swore he hadn't been anywhere near the neighborhood in question. As if he'd admit to anything else.

My guess was Frank, Sam's esteemed father, had hung out at their old residence for a day or so, watching for their return. When they didn't show, he staked out Julia's work, tailing the two buses she rode back to the apartment I'd put her up in. Then he'd cruised by, letting her know she'd been found, letting her know he could hurt her any time he chose. It was another form of control. That was what all fists and the bruises they left behind really were—reminders as to who called the shots.

"I don't care what he said," Julia was saying. "It was him."

"I know. I believe you. But since we don't have any confirmation he broke the restraining order, they have no reasonable cause to go pick him up." I rubbed my eyes. They felt gritty and sore. "They're going to check his cell records, see if his phone pinged off any nearby towers."

"How long will that take?"

"I don't know. Maybe days."

Julia laughed but her eyes swam. "And he could come back here tonight, and I'd be dead tomorrow." She dabbed the napkin at her blackened eye, which was now closer to a deep yellow, and paced to the sliding door, looking out to the backyard where Sam played. "He's barely left that sandbox since we got here. He loves it." She was quiet for a time. "Maybe it would be better," she said without turning around.

"What?"

"If I went back to him. Things would go back to what they were before. Even if he did end up killing me, he would never hurt Sam. He loves Sam."

I put a hand on her shoulder, turning her toward me. "How long do you think he'd hold off from hitting Sam if you went back to him? A year? Two? Maybe not until he was a teenager and had a disagreement with his old man?"

Julia looked away. "What other choice do I have? He won't ever leave us alone."

I glanced around, weighing something out. "Gather up your things."

"What? Why?"

"Because we're leaving."

"Where are we going?"

I watched Sam catch a falling leaf from the air and plant it like a flag on the top of the mound of sand he'd built up.

"Somewhere safe."

At least I hoped it was.

———

If Merrill loved meeting me after being gone for the day, it was nothing compared to welcoming a young boy into our home.

As we walked into the house, Merrill paused at the sight of Julia and Sam behind me, then sprinted forward, his whole body wagging. He'd become a fur-covered wiggle. Sam laughed and knelt in the entryway, accepting Merrill's affection with delighted giggles while Julia examined the broken doorjamb. "I'm remodeling," I said, hanging my coat up.

The notion I was removing them from the frying pan and placing them into the fire had crossed my mind more than once on the drive home. Would whoever ransacked my place come back, or now that they knew I didn't have the iPad, was my house safe again? There was no way of knowing, but I had nothing else to offer Julia and Sam at the moment. It would have to do for now.

While Julia got them settled in the spare bedroom, I opened a bottle of wine and poured two glasses. Sam looked around the openness of the house with wide eyes before asking if he could take Merrill outside. Sure. Of course. Just stay close.

Julia freaked a little when she came out of the bedroom and Sam wasn't nearby. Then I showed her onto the deck overlooking the backyard where the boy and the dog frolicked. There was no other word for it. Jumping, laughing, barking, running. Frolicking. I handed Julia her glass of wine, and she burst into tears.

We settled into two chairs, and I let her cry, not making too much of it. When she'd quieted, I clinked her glass with my own, and we both drank. The wind nudged the trees, and the sun slanted low across the ocean.

"It's so beautiful," Julia finally said. "Your place is gorgeous."

"Thanks. It's my sanctuary. And yours."

"I don't . . ." She set down her wine and sat straighter, facing me. "Why are you doing this?"

"I'll tell you what, let's not dig too deep. I wanted to, that's the gist of it."

"But I don't understand."

"Sometimes good things don't need to be understood."

We drank and listened to the trees talk. Sam threw a stick, and Merrill ran to retrieve it like it was his sole purpose in the universe.

"My sister," Julia said after a while. "She lives in Idaho. Married, nice house in a good neighborhood. Husband has steady work. When I called her a while back and told her what Frank had done—was still doing—know what she said? 'Just leave.' Like it's as simple as that." She laughed, and it sounded like the wine was doing its job. "Leave. I've got a mortgage, a job. No car. Sam has school. How are we supposed to just leave? She's never lived paycheck to paycheck. Never took a punch from someone she loved. But, you know . . . just leave." She whispered the last two words.

"It comes down to help," I said. "A lot of people like to pretend they never needed help, never got it, but that's bullshit. Almost no one gets anywhere without help. And it's the first thing people forget once they get where they're going."

"Come to think of it, that's the one thing my sister didn't offer," Julia said. "She told me to leave, but she didn't say, 'Come stay with us,' or, 'Do you need anything?'" She paused for a moment, staring off into the middle distance. "You wonder what you did wrong. Always. You pore over your mistakes and try to find where things started to fall apart. You want someone to blame, even if it's yourself."

We fell quiet, watching Sam and Merrill play like they'd never run out of energy. Eventually they did and came up to the deck, sweating and panting and asking for something to drink. We all went inside, and while Merrill lapped at his water bowl and Sam downed most of a soda in a few gulps, I refilled Julia's wineglass and told her they could shower while I started dinner. Before she left the kitchen Julia clasped me in a tight hug. For a second I stiffened, completely surprised. Then the warmth of her embrace overwhelmed me, and I hugged her back.

"Thank you," she said in my ear. "You'll never know how much this means to us."

I tried to say it was okay. Tried to say she was welcome, but nothing came out. I settled for nodding and telling her where I kept the extra bath towels.

While they cleaned up I made some calls and started the food. A few times I caught myself wondering what I was doing, asked myself the same question Julia had. I'd always strived to be the best at what I did, but I'd also tried keeping my personal and work life separate. Until now. Because something had shifted when the Volks' plane went down, something inside me, something irrevocable. It felt like there was no way to get back to where I'd been before, and in the end, did I really want to?

Dinner was steak stir fry with fresh side salad. Normally my meals were lower key, but I couldn't resist indulging a bit. Julia and Sam ate with gusto, and I even found myself going back for seconds. Definitely the most I'd eaten in the last week in one sitting. Watching them eat and smile, seeing Julia really relax for the first time since I'd met her, was like standing in front of my success board. But so much better.

When we were finished Julia insisted on her and Sam doing the dishes. His mother washed while Sam dutifully dried, pausing every so often to give Merrill a few pets. I received a text confirmation from one of my prior calls and sent up a quiet thanks.

"This is wonderful, but the only thing is I have no way of getting to work in the morning," Julia said after they'd finished the dishes.

"A rental is getting dropped off later tonight," I said.

She was quiet for a beat, reconciling. "No. No, you can't do that."

"It's already done."

"But how much will that cost?"

"Less than you'd think," I said, grinning as Sam fled from Merrill down the hall only to reappear seconds later near the entry—a blur of boy and dog in a loop, all smiles and lolling tongue.

"I'll pay you back," Julia said, sitting down beside me at the table.

"Let's not worry about that right now. Besides, I have an idea, and if it works, you'll only need the rental for a couple of days at most." Julia frowned while I filled her in on the calls I'd made. As it all sunk in she slowly brightened, like a rheostat on a lamp being turned up.

"It would be like a new beginning for us," she said quietly. Just as quickly the light went out of her features. "He still loves his father," she said after a pause, watching Sam and Merrill cruise past again. "But he also knows daddy hurts mommy. It's been really . . . really hard on him." Tears threatened to overspill her eyes.

"If there's one thing I've learned, it's kids are resilient," I said. "So much more than they should have to be." I took her hand and squeezed it. "You'll both get through this."

My phone chimed a text. A message from a number I didn't recognize floated on the screen.

Nora, this is Taylor. I need to tell you something. Can you meet me at Glenfield Park in an hour?

There was a pause while I processed this. Then another text came through.

Please. I'm afraid.

27

There are hundreds of creeks and rivers flowing outward from the mountains.

Hundreds of streams, all part of vascular tributaries networking toward the sea. Sitka Creek was unaptly named since it fell firmly in the territory of a river. Maybe when whoever had christened it saw it, the water had been placid, ambling along between its banks in search of the Pacific. Now it raged.

It was audible even when turning off the main street onto the park's lookout drive, a dull roar that could've been background static on the radio and which grew exponentially as the trail switchbacked once before emptying out in a wide parking lot hemmed by trees. To the south the land fell away steeply, its canyon dropping in short rocky levels toward the water below. A guardrail, looking quite insignificant compared with the vista, lined the edge of the lot. I nosed my car up to the rail and shut it off, listening to millions of gallons of water race by somewhere below in the dark.

Taylor had answered a few of my questions via text. She was safe but needed to meet urgently. When I asked what it was about, her answer had been simply, *Andrea.*

For a while as I readied to leave the house, telling Julia I'd be gone for just a few hours and to help herself to anything else they needed, Taylor's request had been a quandary. Then it wasn't. Glenfield Park was a short walk from her house, and I hadn't gotten the impression she or her father owned a vehicle. The park's lookout was also one of many make-out spots for the young and amorous in the area. Those who grew up in the city or around it had no shortage of romantic hideaways—a few abandoned movie theaters, a defunct strip mall on the outskirts of town, and many remote lookouts like the one I sat looking at now. Taylor was young and had probably frequented this spot when she was still in high school. I assumed another reason for meeting here was that her father was home, and she didn't feel comfortable having me stop by the house. Even so, the fear in her texts had infected me, and I'd packed a small can of mace.

There were two light poles hunched over the lot, only one of them functional. It spewed a sullen glow on the parking spaces directly beneath it but not any farther. A single vehicle sat in the northwest corner of the lot, but the thick layer of dust and two flat tires said it had been here a long time.

I walked the perimeter of the lot while I waited, the night cool and blustery. A cascade of sodden leaves fell and swirled past, some flying up and out over the drop past the guardrail. A small trail wound down and away at the southwest corner of the lookout leading to the patchy openings in the scrub lining the river gorge where couples migrated if they really wanted to get down to business. I knew this from experience that seemed so old it felt as if I'd gained it in another lifetime.

Standing at the yawning dark and listening to the river, my thoughts strayed. What was I doing here? I leaned against the guardrail. A few seconds later a small figure joined me.

Paul was indistinct, a vagueness in the low light to my left. Looking directly at him would have banished his presence the way movement out of the corner of your eye always disappears the moment you look, only returning when you quit paying attention.

"I'm not forgetting you," I said, despite the fact Paul's definition had been steadily eroding since the last time I'd seen him. I couldn't recall which of his lower teeth he'd lost around the time our mother left. Couldn't remember if he'd always mispronounced *salmon* or *February*. He'd tied his shoes a certain way, but was it making one loop, then wrapping the other lace around it, or forming two bows, then crossing them?

It isn't fair we lose the ones we love twice.

A stick snapped somewhere off in the woods. An animal going about its business or a tree shifting in a gust of wind. At the far end of the lot, someone moved along a walking trail with their dog straining on a leash. Then they faded into the thicker woods surrounding the park. I considered going back to the car to get my phone and text Taylor again but decided to give her a little longer.

She was going to tell me who Andrea had been seeing. That was what all this was about. It had to be. She'd been lying about knowing who it was, we both knew it, and now something had changed.

I'm afraid. That made two of us.

What had happened since visiting her the prior week? Had she spoken to someone? Told the mysterious person Andrea had been seeing about my questions? Or had someone been following me and approached her? Threatened her? She could've gone to the police but had texted me instead. Maybe she was bringing someone with her who needed to speak to me as well. Needed to meet face-to-face. I patted the mace in my pocket absently. It definitely wasn't a message I'd been expecting. If someone had placed a gun to my head, I would've said the card I gave her with my number on it was in the next morning's trash.

For a second there was a strange aligning. The memory of handing Taylor my card paired with the elation of finding Paul's medal the night before. Strange. The two things didn't seem to have any relation at all. Yet something kept tying them together each time I separated them.

Over the rush of the river another twig snapped off in the woods, but this time it sounded closer. Less like the natural shifting of a branch, but more purposeful. Like a footstep.

My car was fifty yards away, its outline a sense of security. Of comfort. Though having my phone in the customary place of my back pocket would've been better. Except why was my heartbeat picking up speed, why really? Because of noises in the woods that was full of small animals? Or because the residue of having someone desecrate my home, my sanctuary, was still so fresh.

The card. The medal. The card. The medal.

Was that a car turning into the lot? No. Just the wind. How late was Taylor now? Five minutes? Ten? Had I possibly gotten confused about the meeting place or time? Had she?

The earlier background noise of traffic on the highway a mile east now seemed very distant. I searched for the dog walker or another person on a late-evening stroll, anything to help stabilize the panicky wobble in my center that was growing exponentially.

The Card. The medal. The card, the medal, the card, the medal, thecardthemedalthecardthemedal—

Those seconds of revelation—so profound they rob you of all other thought. You're exposed to such a high concentration of understanding you're both exhilarated and furious at yourself for not knowing sooner. This particular realization came in the form of a cold stone sinking through my center.

My business cards had been scattered on the floor near the couch where the medal was hiding. All those cards lying there. All of them with my cell number on them.

My feet were already moving toward the car, carrying the rest of my stupid self along while it was still agog with revelations. With *consequences*.

Movement came from the opposite tree line, something not jiving with the nodding branches and fluttering leaves. I slowed, squinting in the gloom.

Someone stepped out of the woods.

28

There was nothing but the swimming night near the trees, then a shadow emerging from it.

They didn't hesitate—the half moment of wondering if it were a homeless person or someone who had gotten turned around in the woods vanished as they headed straight toward me, moving swiftly. Moving with a single-mindedness.

Two more steps were all I needed to know I'd never reach the car before them.

A loosening in my middle almost froze me in place. The deep, real fear that tears through your stomach and leaves you feeling like your insides aren't inside anymore. It pins you down, tries to override fight or flight.

I fought through it and spun, running full tilt back the way I'd come. Back toward the end of the railing I'd been standing at seconds ago feeling alone but safe. I listened over my own footfalls to see if I could hear theirs. A fraction of hope remained that this was some strange misinterpretation and the person from the woods was standing dumbstruck watching me run. I glanced over my shoulder.

They were behind me. Closer.

The sound of their feet crackling the lot's grit, the swish of their clothing. A new bold lance of terror impaled me. They were going to catch me and do terrible things to me here in the dark above the river. They'd lured me here and were going to take exactly what they wanted.

The thought made me dizzy. It gave me adrenaline wings.

I skidded around the end of the guardrail, not slowing to find footing on the path leading down into the scrub. Only running. Silently praying my shoes wouldn't slip or a hole wouldn't turn my ankle. The path was uneven and much steeper than I remembered. For a horrifying second I was falling, then my feet connected with the solidness of rock. My half-adjusted night vision picked out a span of stones like rudimentary stairs, and I flew down them. At the bottom the brush closed in and the path became a 'T'.

Left. Ducking below overhanging branches reaching like hands wanting to grasp and hold me back. A stick snapped behind me, all too close. The trail jagged to the right, straying nearer to the drop beside the river.

Hide, a voice in my head commanded. *Dive into the brush and lie still.* Great plan if I could put some distance between us. Because right now they were close enough to hear them breathing. I poured on speed, calling up all the hikes and workouts I'd ever done. Unknowingly they'd all been for this moment. Another part of me willed the path to lead back toward the parking lot and my waiting car instead of to the river. Memories of cliff jumping into the Sitka's deepest eddies came and went, the exposed rocks and swirling water. It had been dangerous and stupid then, and now the thought of falling from the edge in the dark without knowing what was below became a fresh barb of fear.

An alley flashed by to the right, exposing a small clearing. Closer to the river meant fewer directions to move. Fewer options to hide. The ground rose then dipped, and I stumbled, barely keeping upright before angling hard to the left where another opening appeared.

Something stabbed me in the chest.

A low-hanging branch. It was stout enough to stop my forward progress and spin me sideways. It felt like I'd been punched by a hot fist. All the air left my lungs and I fell, stumbling beneath the heavier growth to my knees, then my belly where I lay with my head pressed into the dirt, panting as silently as I could. Pain radiated outward from my chest with each heartbeat. I was bleeding, I could feel it.

Heavy footsteps pounded closer. Fast.

Keep going.

They neared the opening.

Please keep going.

They slowed.

Stopped.

Fuck.

As loud as my breathing sounded, theirs was louder. A light sprang on and began stabbing through the closest trees.

I rose, low and soundless, skittering to the side, but a boulder halted my progress. Backward took me into deeper grass and fallen leaves, which would whisper and crackle. Forward would put me in their lap. Slowly I drew the mace from my pocket.

The light swung away, and through the foliage a shadow loomed. They were outlined but featureless. A shape in the dark. They could've been anyone. They pivoted, bringing the light around in a half circle. Closer and closer to where I crouched.

My fist tightened on the mace, readying myself for what was to come. Because I was going to have to fight. And I would. An idea suddenly sprang to the forefront of my mind, and my free hand went to my pocket and drew out what was there.

The light's edge cut a few feet to the right, almost revealing my shoe.

I fumbled my keys, almost dropping them.

They took a step closer.

I hit the lock button on my key fob.

Somewhere above us my car chirped its signal. The light froze.

A second. Two.

The light went out, and they were hurrying away, shoes scratching on rock, back in the direction they'd come. I listened for another heartbeat, then sagged, sucking in deep breaths. I wanted to laugh. I wanted to vomit. I had to move. The little stunt might've bought me a few minutes, maybe more. One of two things would happen now—they would either get spooked and run, afraid I either had or would call for help, or they'd come back down the trail after seeing I wasn't anywhere near my car.

Move.

Up on my feet and out into the open feeling like hunted and frightened prey. The river rushed on, blanketing every sound other than my own footsteps and the blood surging in my ears. If they returned, I wouldn't know until they were right on top of me.

My left hand became a fist, keys poking from between knuckles, and I thought of Taylor, who had done the same when I'd approached her. Blood trickled down my chest and onto my stomach. Touching the wound gave me no idea of how severe it was, only that it hurt.

Moving opposite the way they'd gone, I sidled along the trail, head on a swivel, trying to see everywhere at once. After a dozen steps or so the path narrowed, narrowed, ended in a peninsula dropping away to the river. Opposite the ledge, a high shelf of rock led upward in the general direction of the parking lot.

For a second I considered retracing my steps and taking a chance on encountering whoever had chased me. I could thread my way through the woods on the other side of the lookout until I hit the open picnicking areas of the park. But the underbrush would slow me down, would make noise as I went through it. And I'd still be on foot, still be a half mile or more away from the closest neighborhood. I hesitated another heartbeat, and then I was tucking away my keys and mace and climbing the rock shelf, finding handhold after handhold, pulling myself up. Sand and bits of rock sifted down as I moved. The vertical stone angled slightly, and I was able to lean my weight against the wall and rest, breathing hard.

Sweat sheeted down my back. How much farther? Should I wait here or go back? Another five counts of breathing, then upward again.

The incline leveled off, and the parking lot came into view. The guardrail was ten paces away, on its other side—my car.

The rest of the lot was empty. Or seemed to be. I kept scanning it, waiting for something to move, for someone to spring from the undergrowth and leap at me. But there was nothing. Silence. Stillness.

How would I know if they were gone or just biding their time until I revealed myself? Only one way to find out.

I gathered my remaining strength, planning the moves I'd make and tracing the path to the car. I'd have to be fast. So fast. I brought the mace and keys back out, and my thumb found the unlock button on the fob. I'd hit it when I was past the guardrail. The door would be unlocked when I got there. I'd grab the door handle, pull it open, whip into the seat, slam the door shut—

Something moved behind me.

Even as I started to turn my head a hand grasped my ankle.

A sound came from me—distilled terror, and I reacted. My foot pistoned out, trying to kick away the grip. It held tight, but my shoe connected with something solid. There was a grunt, and I was yanked backward.

We slid together.

First over the slight decline, then faster as the rock wall dropped away. They'd lost their balance and pulled me with them. I frantically reached out to grasp something, and the mace spun free. My fingers closed over a ledge, then tore away.

We fell.

Jagged rock bit into my side. I spun.

They were there for a split second, falling with me—body close enough to smell the tang of sweat. Then we landed on the path, me sprawling flat with the air knocked from my lungs for a second time, my attacker spinning toward the edge of the canyon—then over it.

The ensuing quiet told me a story. There was nothing below the cliff except empty air. No grade to slow their descent. No trees to grasp. Nothing.

Two full seconds passed before a sickening thud and splash came in quick succession. I envisioned a head or shoulder pulverizing on an exposed rock in the river, a crumpled body flipping over into the water, sinking below, then resurfacing. I pictured an arm coming up and grabbing a stone to stop themselves in the current. Battered and bleeding, they would pull themselves toward the shoreline and begin to climb.

I was up and moving without recalling getting to my feet. The path swayed as if it were a rope bridge. I found enough balance to jog. Then run.

The parking lot looked like an oasis—the light cascading from the single lamp a beacon. My keys were ingrained in my palm, having gripped them as I fell, and it took two tries to unlock the door.

Inside the car. Doors locked. Key in ignition. Drive.

As I backed out I kept waiting to see someone claw their way up into view like some kind of killer in a slasher flick. Undying. Unstoppable. But there was nothing. Stillness and the emptiness of the lookout.

I left rubber on the pavement and sped into the night.

29

Update and memorial | Kaylee Volk

550,267 views * Oct 17, 2022

Kaylee Volk (Volks At Home)

2.3M subscribers

AN UPDATE AND MEMORIAL PLAN Thank you all for watching and checking in. I'm officially out of the hospital and resting. A memorial for my family will be livestreamed on Wednesday for those interested—

Video Plays

Kaylee sits on the edge of a king-size bed—the uniform blasé background of a hotel room behind her. There is more life in her eyes, and her injuries are beginning to soften around the edges. Healing.

KAYLEE

Hello, everyone. I wanted to let you all know I've been officially discharged from the hospital.

(a wan smile)

Still having a lot of pain, and it's a long road of recovery ahead, but I feel so much better being out.

She glances around.

KAYLEE

I'm sure you noticed this isn't our . . . this isn't home.

(a long pause)

Honestly I couldn't go back there. At least not yet. I don't know . . . I don't know if I'll ever be able to. The memories might be too much. It would feel too empty without all of them.

Kaylee licks her lips and shifts in her seat, realigning herself.

KAYLEE

I know there are watershed moments in life, where afterward everything is different. Usually they're small and go mostly unnoticed, but sometimes they're like this. They're a gulf that seems uncrossable.

She gathers herself. Tears shine in her eyes.

KAYLEE

Wednesday will be a week since the crash. Since I lost everything. I'm still having trouble reconciling that they're gone. I've been in touch with my therapist, and she says the first step of grief is accepting grief itself. She said to begin that journey any way that felt right to me.

She blinks back tears and smiles sadly.

KAYLEE

So on Wednesday at 7:00 p.m. Pacific, I'll be doing a livestream at the beach where we took the kids swimming all those times. I'll be setting four wreaths on the water in their memory.

(a beat)

Yes, four. I don't know why Andrea did what she did, and maybe I'll never know, but what I won't do is hold hatred in my heart for her. She was a tortured young woman who did something monstrous, but she was suffering too. And now she's gone.

Kaylee looks around again as if trying to recognize something in the anonymous setting.

KAYLEE

The way forward for me isn't clear, but I'm so thankful to have your continual support and love. Knowing you're all on the other end of these posts is what's been keeping me sane the last week, so thank you, and goodbye for now.

Video Ends

30

There was a closed gas station two miles from the park where I pulled over to throw up.

The intervening time between escaping and the moment my dinner suddenly needed to be free of me was dreamlike. I'd driven too fast, then found myself coasting, foot off the gas, thoughts racing and carrying me a thousand miles away. The gas station itself was dark, but its parking lot was well lit. I pulled off, climbed from the car, and was violently sick in the grass hemming the cracked concrete.

A few cars passed while I shakily regained my bearings. The night was cool and clear. It was almost like the universe was trying to cover up what had happened. The insanity of the last half hour just a speed bump. Life went on. Or it almost hadn't for me, but that didn't seem to matter. The crickets sang and the breeze still blew.

I drove to the hospital. My injuries had clotted, but throwing up might've been pure nerves or a brain bleed. I didn't want to chance going home without making sure, even though it was the only place I wanted to be.

While I got checked in, I explained to the nurse I'd been attacked and needed her to call the police and have someone meet me here. She was young, and her eyes were large and round as she took in my bloody shirt and picked up the phone to do as I asked. The doctor who examined me was older and gruff, a veteran of the night shift who listened more than he talked. He ordered a CAT scan and inspected my wounds. *You'll make it*, he said with a half smile. While we waited for the test results, a nurse cleaned and dressed my cuts. None of them needed stitches, but the antiseptic was enough to bring stinging tears to my eyes.

A detective knocked on my exam room door a while later. Her name was Susan Tern, and she was short with a bob cut of blonde hair framing her shrewd features. She mimicked the ER doctor and mostly listened to me tell her what happened, interjecting a question only every so often. No, I didn't see their face. No, they hadn't said anything, so I had no idea what their voice might sound like. Could I think of anyone who wanted to harm me?

The last one gave me pause. Detective Tern watched me hesitate, phone held out in one hand recording our conversation. No, I couldn't say who would want to hurt me. She nodded but didn't press any further. A couple more questions, and then she said she'd have a patrol stationed outside my house for the next few nights. She'd start a trace on the cell number that had texted me. If we were lucky, it was a burner phone bought recently at a major retailer and there would be surveillance tape or a receipt with a name on it. If we were lucky.

I didn't feel lucky, and I knew I was the luckiest person in the world. When we'd fought we might not have fallen the way we did, and I might be lying dead right now on that path below the overlook. Or they could've caught me and done whatever it was they wanted. My mother used to say we made our own luck. I guess I'd made mine.

"Call me if you think of anything else," Tern said before going out the door. *Call if you want to tell me the truth*, was the message her eyes conveyed.

The CAT scan was clear. The doctor double-checked my dressings and asked if I needed anything else. He walked me to the lobby and patted me once on the back, saying to take it easy for the next few days. Byron was waiting near my car when I went outside.

He was in civilian clothes, his normally smoothed hair in disarray. He watched me approach and looked me over as if checking for any visible injuries.

"Are you okay?" he said.

"Yeah." A beat. "Who told you?"

"Someone in dispatch who took the call from the hospital." He shook his head. "Don't blame them, they didn't know we aren't—" He winced. "What the hell happened?"

I sighed and told him, basically repeating the conversation with Detective Tern. When I mentioned the text messages and whoever was masquerading as Taylor, he stiffened and looked off across the mostly empty parking lot. When I finished, we were both quiet. A silent ambulance left the hospital garage and glided away into the dark.

"Someone's been following you," he said after a while.

"I would assume."

"Jesus! How can you be so casual about this?" He was angry, outraged on my behalf. I felt numb. I just wanted to go home.

"I'm processing," I said.

He held out his hands. "Okay, and I'm not saying this to interfere, but you need to stop whatever you're doing. I know you don't want my help, but at least listen to me. Please stop."

"I think it was Justin Volk," I said.

We were suspended for a second, like we'd been hoisted a few inches off the ground, then dropped. "What?" he said.

"I think Justin Volk survived the crash. I think he's the one who's been following me and broke in."

"Nora, listen—"

"I spoke to his father, and he said Justin hated his foster kids. Maybe Kaylee was confused. Maybe it was him instead of Andrea who crashed the plane. Maybe—"

"Justin is dead."

"Really? Did they find his body?"

Joe Hart

"No, but they found Andrea's."

I faltered, the seconds fracturing and stretching out. "When?"

"Earlier today." Byron sighed and ran a hand through his hair, messing it up further. "She'd drifted a long way south and washed up. She was . . . pretty damaged." He glanced around, then focused on me again, his voice quieter. "I don't know what's going on because you won't tell me, and I don't know who's after you, but it's not Justin Volk. It was an absolute miracle Kaylee survived. Justin's body will wash in just like Bethany's and Andrea's."

I put a hand against my car to steady myself.

My head swam.

Nothing made sense.

Everything I'd learned was untethered and awash, all the facts mixed together in a miasma of confusion. And through it came the painful stab of picturing Andrea's body beached somewhere. Damaged and degraded. All her life's potential snuffed out, leaving only a sad husk behind as proof she'd existed.

"I need to go home," I heard myself say. Byron didn't reply. He stood there by my car, his head down, eyes fixed on the asphalt at his feet. He was still standing there when I pulled away.

———

Home. A police cruiser was stationed near the end of my drive, and I gave the officer inside a quick wave. Upon pulling into the driveway I was at a loss for a second seeing a strange car parked there, then remembered Julia's rental had been dropped off.

Inside everything was quiet. The guest-room door was open a few inches. Julia had built Sam a fort bed on the floor, where he snored softly. She lay sprawled beneath the covers next to him, an arm stretched out in his direction. I pulled the door fully shut.

A long shower, the water as hot as I could stand it. It meant rebandaging myself, but it was so worth it. Clean aching body and clean clothes, I settled into my chair and stared out the tall windows at the night.

Was the person who'd chased me out there right now, on their way here, hungry for a second try? Or were they a corpse washing quickly down the Sitka, another secret to be revealed at some later time? There was no way to know, but the fall had been significant, along with the meaty sound of impact. Their body drifting in the current became Andrea's. Her eye shadow traded for bruised flesh, the scar on her cheek eaten by fish. She beckoned, reached out for me, cold, briny fingers touching my face.

I snapped awake, unaware I'd drifted off. I double-checked all the doors, only then noticing a particular aspect of returning home had been missing. I found Merrill asleep in his bed at the foot of mine, snores mimicking Sam's as his side rose and fell. He'd been completely worn out. It brought a tired smile to my face.

In bed sleep wouldn't come. Everything hurt. The sheets were sandpaper, and my temp fluctuated from hot to cold to hot again. Each time I managed to drift off, my nerves would slingshot me back awake. Wash, rinse, repeat.

Near dawn I went under for good and stayed there. A looping dream ran endlessly through my sleeping mind. Crawling up the side of the drop-off, a hand coming out of the dark and grabbing me, falling, landing hard enough to fracture bones and beginning to climb again. Over and over and over.

Merrill woke me, his nose pressed into the side of my face. I blearily waved him away, wanting more sleep. Except the light was slanting in the room the wrong way. It took three blinks to see clearly enough and confirm the time on my phone. It was 1:00 p.m. I'd slept all morning and part of the afternoon.

Climbing from bed was an experiment in pain. Every joint was a rusted hinge, my muscles aching harp strings. They loosened a little in another boiling shower. The lacerations from the night before had acquired parhelion bruises, which glowed angrily from beneath fresh gauze. Merrill watched me dress as if it were my first time. "I'm all messed up," I said after finally donning a second sock. He gazed back as if to say, *Tell me something new.*

The house was empty and the rental was gone. Good. Julia would've been all questions at seeing my appearance, and I had less than zero will to explain. Besides, she needed to be at work today to execute our plan. I checked the time again; still a few hours before I had to leave. My appetite was a shriveled thing in my center, but I managed to force down a couple of eggs and some toast.

As I sat sipping a second cup of coffee, I noticed a hand-shaped bruise forming on my calf, and a wave of panic washed over me so strongly, I had to brace myself in the chair and wait for it to pass. Gradually it receded, and my breathing returned to something closer to normal. Since my father, no one had lain hands on me in anger. There'd been a few attempts during child removals, but nobody had ever broken that threshold I'd built for myself over the years.

Until now.

I rocked in place, trying to quell the electric sickness in my stomach. Being a child of abuse was a little like trying to outrun a storm. For a time you're caught directly in the tempest, then—if you're lucky—you escape it. But you're never really free. You can see the shadow on the ground behind you on sunny days. You know if you hesitate or make the wrong move, you'll be fully back under its cover, feeling cold rain and pounding wind. All you ever want to do is stay ahead of the storm.

My phone chimed a text, and it sent a ripple of gooseflesh across my skin. Would it be from the same number as last night? Some new threat or promise of violence, an answer to whether or not they'd survived the drop? I relaxed slightly seeing it was from Tracy Jenkins at work.

Hi, Nora. Kaylee Volk called trying to reach you. I wanted to check with you before passing on her contact info. She said it was important.

31

Kaylee's hotel was a block down from the building where my father had massacred his coworkers.

I rarely came to this part of town. Not because I couldn't deal with seeing his sniper's perch or the parking lot where the bodies had fallen, but because I didn't like to. Who would? Seeing the place where he'd unleashed death upon so many others and then himself was just another reminder his blood flowed in my veins. I avoided it like I avoided writing my last name when I could get away with it. Seeing it created by my own hand felt like an offense. A doctor had once suggested changing my name, creating a break and a fresh start, a new identity all my own. I'd considered it, thought about it for weeks, then dismissed the idea. Shedding his name would've been like painting over rotten wood. It was temporary, and what was underneath always came bubbling to the surface.

Kaylee had been brief on the phone, saying she needed to see me, to discuss something in person if possible. She'd rented out a suite near the top of the hotel and asked me to please keep it confidential—there were people who would pay good money to find where she was staying. Some were reporters while others were doom seekers—people who fed off tragedy and only wanted to be close to the fallout of such events. Maybe the two were one and the same sometimes.

A man in a tight T-shirt answered my knock. He was slabbed with years of gym muscle, and a Taser of some fashion rested on one hip. I told him who I was, and he nodded, stepping aside, but not before checking the hall to make sure I was alone.

The suite was wide, with expansive views of the city. A sunken living area with three leather couches and a chair anchored the space. Kaylee sat at the end of the nearest couch and rose when I stepped into the room.

She was dressed in leggings and a loose designer sweater. Her feet were bare. Here was the woman most resembling the Kaylee from before. She'd applied makeup, which hid most of the fading bruises, and her hair swept down over one shoulder in a gold curtain. Besides her casted arm being in a sling, she might've just stepped out of one of her videos.

"Nora, thanks so much for coming." She clasped one of my hands in her own in an awkward reverse handshake. Then, over my shoulder, she said, "Bill, we're fine. You can go grab lunch." Her security nodded, and a few seconds later the door clicked shut. "Sit, please," Kaylee said, motioning to the single chair. "Tea?" she asked as we settled into our seats. A small pot steamed next to two cups.

"No, thank you."

"It's a special blend I buy online. I really missed it in the hospital," she said, pouring a cup before tucking her legs beneath her on the couch. She looked so small and young, she could've been a teenager instead of in her midtwenties. I waited. Kaylee sipped her tea and set it down. "So I wanted to apologize for the last time we spoke. I kind of lost it there at the end."

"It's okay. You don't need to be sorry."

She watched me as if to see if I were being genuine or polite. "Thank you. You're really the only person I've talked to other than the police and a few reporters."

"Your family hasn't . . ."

"My sister's publicist checked in." She breathed a laugh. "And my brother called to complain about you."

I struggled for a second. "I'm sorry, I wanted to learn more was all and—"

"Don't apologize. Evan and my relationship is . . . complicated. Prison changed him, mostly for the better, which is great. But in some ways it's become a wedge too. I couldn't bear seeing him in there, but I wrote him constantly and got reports from the warden's administration. But Evan didn't understand and—" She grimaced. "It's been hard."

I thought of Stephen and me, the easy bond we shared, an undercurrent we both swam in, and was deeply grateful for it. Sometimes trauma is a knife, sometimes it's stitches. "He said you hadn't really spoken," I offered.

"Did he mention anything else?"

"Like?"

"I don't know. I guess I'm trying to make sense of everything. That's really why I asked you here."

I shifted in my seat, thinking I would tell her I'd been put on administrative leave, then said, "I'll help if I can."

Kaylee gave me a smile and sipped her tea. "I'm sure you know about my family, the history. It was rough growing up in all the . . . scandal. I didn't really understand it at the time. When I was older, I realized what a lot of the rumors and talk behind my back was about. It affected me. I didn't know how to process it." She smiled coldly and stared at something across the room. "Natalie had her acting, and Evan had his drugs. I didn't have much of anything except time to wonder why I was alone. Then I met Justin, and everything was different. And now everything's different again." Her gaze came back to me. "You know about that, though. How it all can change in a heartbeat."

The gyroscope in my center swayed. "Yes. I do."

"That's why I hoped you could help me understand why Andrea did this. I want . . . I need to know what happened to her. What would drive her to do this to us."

I sat forward, knowing the next bit was akin to high-wire walking. "You told me Justin was acting strange, like he was drunk, after takeoff, and that Andrea pushed the controls down. Do you think anything else could've been happening right then?"

"What do you mean?"

"Traumatic incidents are . . . unique in how the mind identifies and encodes a memory. In high-stress situations things can get warped or seem different than what they were."

She watched me. Her shoulders had drawn up tighter, and her posture straightened. "You think I'm mistaken."

"I didn't say that. I'm saying the brain rejects certain things sometimes that we don't want to accept." For a second I saw the bundle of clothes lying in a wedge of light, knowing they were Paul's clothes, knowing it was Paul inside them, but unable to believe it was him. That he was gone.

"So what are you saying?"

"Is there any chance Justin might've made a mistake? Could he have—"

"No. No, I know what I saw," Kaylee said. Her voice grated slightly. "I was there, I lived it. Andrea crashed the plane. I tried to stop her. That's it."

"Okay," I said, holding out a hand. "I believe you."

Kaylee looked out the window. She was quiet for a beat. "That's the building over there, isn't it?"

I followed her gaze. Sat looking at it for a moment. "Yes."

"I read about your family too. It only seemed fair. It was horrible, what he did." She said it without malice. A statement, a matter of fact. It was how I'd approached the vile act my father committed over the years since. It was horrendous. People died. My father died. My brother

165

died. But there was no real meaning in it. It's the cold truth so hard to accept. Tragedy should mean something, but mostly it doesn't. Some people were broken, and they broke others. The ones left behind picked up the pieces and carried on. If they could. There was heartache and damage, but we carried on. Still, Kaylee mentioning it now stirred the hairs on my neck and arms.

"It was," I said, keeping my voice steady.

"Do you know why?"

A long silence. "No."

"Don't you want to?"

"No. He was a sick man. It happened a long time ago."

Kaylee seemed transfixed by the building where my father had worked, where he had killed and died. "Have you forgiven him?"

"No."

"Could you? Could you forgive someone who did something that awful?"

I rubbed a hand against my eyebrow. My head hurt. "I guess I've made my peace with it."

Kaylee finally faced me again. "I'm glad," she said after a time. "But I don't think I'll ever be able to do that. I said on my last video I don't hate her. That's not true. I do. I do hate her. I hate what she took from me." She swiped at one eye. "I have to know why she did it. Will you help me?"

The city churned on outside. Kaylee waited. I gave her an answer.

32

Julia Roust worked as a head housekeeper for a low-end chain of motels.

She'd started at the bottom when she was twenty, toiling away behind a supply cart and cleaning up guests' shit and piss for eight or ten hours a day for five years before the former head of housekeeping retired, vacating the position for someone younger. It was a small step up, Julia had told me, but a vital one. One that provided a bit more pay and a little less time on her knees scrubbing grout in bathrooms. She said she'd gladly work as long as she could support Sam, always on the lookout for a better position somewhere else while never finding it.

I sat in my car looking at the motel, the faded blue vinyl siding, the weeds in the transition strip between the sidewalk and parking lot. This was a family's salvation. A place Julia came to and worked away the hours of her life to live the free time with her son. It was pure and simple dedication that made my throat close off. A million other families did the same—worked dead-end jobs at places just like this, but this was theirs.

Julia's rental sat at the far end of the lot amid a collection of other employee vehicles. I'd parked a dozen or so spaces away in a good vantage to take in the highway and turnaround that swept into and behind the motel. I was early, and that was good since I hadn't planned on sleeping so late or visiting Kaylee.

Kaylee.

I'd said yes. As if there'd been any other choice. As if I hadn't already been doing exactly what she was asking. It felt like permission. Like validation. That this whole thing wasn't water under a bridge like everyone in my life wanted it to be, like they told me it was. In a strange way Kaylee and I were connected. Almost . . . alike. Both from broken homes, both in foster care, both victims of tragedy. And now allies in this oddly twisting story playing out in real time.

It wasn't over.

That was the sentiment that kept rising every so often in the back of my mind. It bordered upon instinct. All that had happened, it wasn't finished yet. There were still machinations moving beneath the surface, things that could be brought to light if I didn't stop. If I kept going . . .

A nondescript beige sedan pulled into the lot. It cruised slowly past a few rows of guest vehicles before angling in my direction. It stopped when the driver's side was even with mine, and I rolled my window down. The car's occupant did the same.

Abraham Foster sat in the driver's seat. We'd known one another since I'd first joined CPS and he'd been a new-hire sheriff's deputy. We'd met on my very first removal and had been friends since. He was now state police and forever Abe to me.

"Should commission you for my stakeouts. You're even early. You bring snacks? Donuts?" Abe said.

"Stale pretzel bites."

He made a face. "Anything yet?"

"No. You've got the description and plate number?"

He nodded. A brief squawk came from his radio, and he turned it down. Other than the computer module mounted on the dashboard, his unmarked car was inconspicuous—its dullness hurt to look at. "You got a good spot here. Gonna pull around on the other side. You said this guy might be dangerous, right?"

"Could be. His ex thinks he is. I wouldn't have called you otherwise." We looked at the motel for a minute. "Thanks for coming," I said.

168

He waved a hand. "Wasn't busy with anything except my own life. Boring shit and all."

"You don't think you'll need backup?"

"We'll see." He pulled away, swung a tight loop to my other side, and parked.

It was 4:54 p.m. Julia got off in six minutes. I'd prepped her on what to do this afternoon—*Don't look around, and act normal even if you see Frank's car. We'll take it from there.*

The seconds ticked by. I reclined my seat so I wasn't as visible to passersby. Abe had done the same. If Frank was serious about hurting Julia, there was a good chance he'd show up here. Her work was somewhere she couldn't avoid going. If he'd visited the apartment near the courthouse yesterday and realized she and Sam weren't there, he'd need to pick her up again and follow to find her new hideout. It was ballsy given the restraining order against him, but Julia's fear had been the determining factor in calling Abe. She knew her ex better than anyone else, knew what he was capable of. I trusted that fear. I wasn't going to wave away her concerns like so many others did and put faith in the system. There were protections and well-meaning people behind them, but it wasn't enough. The system never seemed to be liable. Never accountable. Just filled with platitudes and protocols that did nothing when the chips were down. It was nowhere to be seen in the aftermath.

The clock ticked over to 4:58 p.m. He wasn't coming. Frank had gotten spooked by the visit from the cops and backed off, biding his time until another day. He'd wait and watch, and when Julia had begun to believe he was moving on, he'd appear in her doorway or at her bedside in the middle of the night. These thoughts went through my mind as a rusted green El Camino glided off the highway and into the lot.

My head snapped around toward Abe, who had sat up slightly. He jutted his chin toward the car. I nodded. The El Camino slid quietly between the rows, slowing at one point before continuing on—a predator prowling in search of a meal. As it got closer Frank's silhouette solidified behind the glass, his crew cut, the wide set of his shoulders. I locked eyes with Abe again, and he brought his seat upright.

Frank drove past us without looking our way. Abe waited for a count of five before pulling out behind him. At the very back end of the lot, Frank swung a quick ninety and reversed into a space, the perfect spot to watch the front door, to wait for Julia to show herself. Abe drove as if to pass Frank by, and at the last second nosed his car into the El Camino's so it had nowhere to go.

Abe hit the hidden lights in the front and back windows. Strobes of blue, red, and white. Frank sat up very straight in his seat. His mouth opened a little, and he glanced around—looked right at my car but didn't see me. He was wondering how this happened. How he could've been spotted and found out. Like he'd been so careful in his plotting when it was the simplest thing in the world to anticipate the thinking of a man like him.

Abe unfolded from his car, all six feet two of him, his bulk sturdy and strong and confident. He rounded his trunk, one hand resting casually on the large pistol strapped to his hip, and made a motion to Frank, who was still frozen behind the steering wheel.

I leaned forward as if to peer ahead in time through these next moments. To see if there would be havoc, if there would be blood. My knuckles were white dots gripping the wheel.

Frank lowered his window, and the murmur of his and Abe's voices floated across the quiet lot. Movement came from the motel entrance as Julia exited right on time. She tried not to glance around; I could see it in her body language. She was dead set on acting so normal that she moved stiffly, like a puppet. She looked up and saw everything. She halted.

"Keep moving," I said. "Go." She did after a second. On the other side of the lot, Abe was ordering Frank out of his car. Frank shook his head, both hands waving in irritation. I could almost hear his complaints. *I wasn't doing anything. I've got rights. This is America.*

Abe drew his weapon.

Julia neared her rental and finally spotted me. I motioned for her to get in the car. She did. Frank was finally following Abe's directions, shoving his door open resignedly.

There was a tipping point where things could've gone differently. Could've gone sideways, where everything came unglued at once. I imagined Frank rushing Abe, Abe firing point blank. I saw a knife flash up and cut Abe from waist to throat. But it passed as Abe slid a set of zip cuffs onto Frank's wrists behind his back, frisked him, and led him to his unmarked car.

Only when the back door was shut and Frank was secure did I relax. I slumped into the seat, realizing I'd been straining forward so hard a laceration on my side had begun weeping blood. I shoved a handful of napkins from the glovebox under my shirt and called it good while Abe donned a pair of latex gloves and began searching Frank's car. Julia had driven to the mouth of the lot and was waiting for a break in traffic to pull out. I was glad. Glad she was facing the opposite direction. Glad she wasn't there to see what I saw.

Abe straightened from inside the El Camino's passenger seat and drew something long and dark into the light.

A rifle.

33

Those branches in time.

The decisions that change the trajectory of life. I let myself wonder sometimes when I wasn't on guard, when the drawbridge of emotions hadn't been raised. I wondered and pinpointed where the junctures were, where each turning point could've made a difference.

Our father could've gotten help. He might've spent time in therapy, tried medications, managed the cold fire burning inside him no one knew was there. Maybe eventually it would have gone out.

Our mother could've taken us away with her wherever she went. I think of some beach house south of the border—she always loved Mexico—of rolling turquoise waves and sand so white it hurts your eyes. Paul and Stephen and I run on the beach and go swimming until our skin is pruny and soft. In time we speak Spanish as well as English.

Paul could've eaten his share of the food. We might've survived. He could be living in a nice house a few miles from me with a wife and two kids. I'd take his children on hikes and teach them how to surf. He and I would sit across from one another in the quiet moments after a good dinner and sip a drink, letting that shared knowledge of survival thrum between us, knowing we'd made it out of something terrible together.

———

I drove around in the evening, not paying attention to where the car took me. It was the twilight hours I felt the most comfortable in, that time where afternoon finally decides to slip toward night. The quality of the light seemed to fill me up, not with happiness or despair, but longing for things to be different. If I could just find how to make them so.

Julia and Sam were back at the apartment near the courthouse. She'd called fifteen minutes or so after Abe had pulled the wicked-looking rifle from Frank's El Camino. She confirmed he was being arrested for violating the restraining order. She wanted to know how long he'd be locked up for. I told her nothing was for certain, but I'd seen multiple other men sentenced to at least six months. No, he wouldn't be out on bail again. She and Sam were safe.

For now were the two words I kept to myself.

There'd been a short pause, and when she came back on the line, her voice was husky with tears. She thanked me. Thanked me for everything I'd done. There was another break, and she laughed, saying Sam was asking if he could come visit Merrill someday soon. I laughed with her and said they were welcome anytime. We hung up with promises to see each other in the next few days. She didn't know about the rifle yet. I didn't tell her. I couldn't.

I took Abe out for a drink, he'd more than earned it. We went to a local dive bar and did a couple shots, each nursing a beer afterward, coming down off the success, off the rush. It was a win, and I was beyond grateful for it. Needed it more than I'd known.

While we chatted I thought how things would've been different if it was Byron sitting across from me instead. I'd considered calling him initially, but the same reservation that kept me from asking him to spend the night after the break-in stayed my hand. I really did like the guy, and I wasn't about to leverage his feelings for something I needed. There was a divide there now, and I wasn't sure if it was still crossable or not.

Later, after cruising aimlessly and finding myself turning into the Volks' neighborhood, I wasn't surprised. I parked across the street from the house and shut the car off. Someone had set up a vigil/shrine on the front stoop others had added to. Electric candles danced around a pile of stuffed animals and carboard signs. Mylar balloons secured to a railing floated halfway to the ground like weary ghosts.

The remembrance of a tragedy and one narrowly averted. Their intersections were palpable, a thinning of the air, something I could almost taste. My stomach was sick from the what ifs of the afternoon. What if Julia hadn't accepted my help? What if I hadn't called Abe? What if we'd waited a day? But none of those had happened. Frank was in jail where he belonged, and Julia and her son could breathe a little easier tonight.

So why couldn't I?

I thought of all the other families, all the other women living in fear who only had the reassurances of the system to go on. But today the system would have failed Julia and her son. If I'd still been bound by the regulations of my profession and hadn't interfered personally, Frank may have used that rifle, and Sam might've lost his mother. Or his life.

I gasped for air and stepped from the car.

Outside the night had taken on a cool clamminess, forcing my jacket zipper to the top. The neighborhood was empty and quiet except for the tinny sound of music coming from somewhere at the street's end. It was darker, and the electric candles on the Volks' steps fluttered as if in response to the breeze.

I approached the house and looked up into its eyes. Kaylee had asked for help. She needed to know why. Standing here in front of the place where the family had spent their lives, it was still so hard to understand. I'd approached it from all angles—selfishly at first, wanting to know if I was culpable somehow, if I hadn't done enough. After that there'd been no stopping. Like Kaylee, I needed to know.

Something moved in the upstairs window.

I blinked and took a step back, unsure of what I'd seen. A reflection of the trees swaying in the wind? A car passing? No, no traffic had gone by while I'd been standing here. Given my state of mind and the previous night's injuries, it might've been my imagination. Jumping at shadows, at nothing.

Except . . .

I withdrew another step from the porch, unable to focus on a single window. They all were too dark, too opaque to see if there was someone there behind them, watching. And it felt like there was. The weight of eyes pressed against my skin like cold fingers and raised a crop of goose bumps. My scalp tightened, hair attempting to stand up.

A flash of the night before consumed me. The figure emerging from the dark woods. Coming straight for me without hesitation. For half a second I saw them again in the Volks' yard, rounding the house at a sprint, hands outstretched.

The street beneath my heels brought me back. I'd retreated without realizing, and still it felt as if someone watched me. Maybe it was the house itself, glowering down, empty and haunted with the echoes of lives no longer within. Or maybe it was something else.

I hurried across the road to my car and locked the door once inside. Leaving the neighborhood I cranked the heat. My house was almost in sight by the time I stopped shivering.

34

Inside. All the doors locked. All the lights on. A little safer.

Merrill greeted me with his usual gusto, though I could sense he was still tired from his and Sam's playtime the day before. "You're not a pup anymore, are you?" I said, scratching him behind the ear. He kicked his back leg in response.

A shower. A change of bandages. Comfy clothes. A glass of wine.

Detective Tern had called while I was in the bathroom. A team of divers had begun sweeping the Sitka River below the park but had yet to find anything. So far tracking down the burner phone's origin had been just as fruitful. She said she would keep me updated and to call if I remembered anything else. I remembered too much, but nothing that would help her find who my attacker was.

PTSD. Intrusive memories. Trauma. Whatever you wanted to call it. That was why I'd fled the Volks' yard. Seeing a reflection in a window was enough to trigger it. I'd had enough of the same reactions when I was younger to know what it was. There was a foreignness to it now, like returning to a strange country where you knew the layout, but some things had changed in your absence. No one had been inside the Volks' house watching me. It was nerves. That was it. That was all.

I needed to think. To step back and survey what I'd learned if I was actually going to help Kaylee come to terms with her loss. She may've been a stereotypical online influencer a week ago, someone to watch with curious disdain or outright scorn, but now she was a victim. Someone I couldn't get myself to dismiss. Someone who needed help.

What did I know?

I knew Kaylee wanted the perfect family. I knew Mason had wanted a good education. Andrea had been seeing someone in secret. Justin may have been using painkillers and hated his foster children. I knew Justin's father was a creep, and Evan Baker wanted to be left completely out of anything having to do with his sister. I knew Taylor was covering for Andrea, even in death, as a true friend would. I knew someone had been following me from the get-go, someone who may have seen me in the Volks' house the night I went in and found the iPad.

The iPad.

I drank the last of my wine. It was what the person at the overlook had been after. Its location. I could come up with no other reason to lure me there. It was also what I hoped would break everything wide open. But there was a part of me that worried I was wrong and it was just a little girl's device. Filled with games and silly pictures and bad digital artwork—the hallmarks of any nine-year-old. But there was something else to consider, the only other clue I had to go on.

The teddy bear.

Its absence could've been anything from a bizarre coincidence to the key to explaining everything. I was beginning to lean toward the latter but couldn't figure out the connection to the iPad. There was something, some maddening link between the two that was just out of reach, but no matter how hard I tried, I couldn't grasp it. Each time I came close it would turn to smoke and fade away.

For now the iPad was my best chance, but Stephen hadn't called or texted since our talk in his kitchen. Not to say yes or no about helping me with the device. It wasn't like him to ignore me or I him, but I couldn't let him know what had happened in the interim. Couldn't let him know about the break-in or the near miss at the park. Couldn't let him know he'd been right.

Shame welled within me. These people in my life, the only family I had left, they all wanted me to be safe, to be happy, to stop. All I had to do was listen to them.

Merrill curled up on the floor, his side leaning heavily on my feet. After a time Paul stood near the windows, not looking out. Looking at me.

I drifted.

Early-morning gray light seeped through the windows. Paul was gone. I shuffled my aching body to bed, Merrill plodding behind me. Sleep again, restless and light. Voices that seemed to come from everywhere at once, but when I surfaced the house was quiet. They were only in my head.

Around noon thunder brought me up to a drowse. Lightning flashed in muted whites and reds through my eyelids as I lay there listening to the storm. When I finally rose, my body was somehow stiffer than the day before if that were possible. It didn't seem fair. A scalding shower and a change of clothes, then a little breakfast watching the rain through slitted eyes.

It was like traveling back in time. A week ago the weather had been the same. Except right now I'd been at work, preparing for the removal of Anita Warren's children. And the Volks had been readying to fly up the coast. Everything hanging in the balance. Everything happening as it was always going to.

I let Merrill finish my breakfast and took some coffee onto the deck. The overhang kept a decent area dry, and I leaned against the siding, watching the trees bend and sway. The ocean was lost in a gray haze, but it was out there, waiting like it had been last week to swallow the aircraft that had plummeted into it. Right now Kaylee would be prepping for her livestream memorial in just a few hours' time. To the average observer it probably looked needy, a ploy for views and attention. Maybe it was. Maybe it was the only way for her to process what had happened. No one got to say how another grieved. There was no right or wrong way. There was only the valley of loss and how you made your way out of it. Some never did.

The doorbell rang and Merrill woofed in response. When I opened the door, Stephen stood hunched in his peacoat, his hair and shoulders dark with rain. He took in the splintered doorframe, how it had been repaired, and shook his head.

"Jesus, Nora. Why the hell didn't you tell me?"

I beckoned him inside.

35

There was a tree in the front yard of our foster parents' home.

In a prior generation it had been an apple tree. It had borne fruit. But with time it aged and gave up its purpose to gnarl in on itself even as it grew taller and thicker at its base.

We climbed it. Its ladderlike branches gave us no other choice. Stephen and I would ascend as high as we dared without drawing the attention of our foster mother or father, then climb a little higher—each time wondering how far we could go before the branches became too thin, too brittle to hold us. We wondered if we climbed high enough if we'd be able to see beyond the horizon, see to a point where our eyes would fail and be lost there in awe.

I remember one day Stephen told me not to go any higher, not to chance the next level where the last of the leaves were beginning to brown from the overnight frosts. I'd looked down through my sneakered feet at his upturned and pleading face and hated him a little. I was the older sibling, the one who made the rules. He was supposed to follow. Paul was gone, and I was the one he looked up to now. It felt heavy to know that. I needed to be brave.

So I called him a name and went upward. Not listening to him say I was going to get hurt. Not caring if I did. Only wanting to reach the top. To know what it looked like from up there.

I don't remember falling. Only the sound of snapping branches and twigs on my descent. The startling speed of gravity. The final and oldest branch kept me from plummeting all the way to the ground, its bulk slamming into my stomach and leaving my lungs feeling like they'd never hold air again.

Stephen helped me down and supported me as I hobbled around the side of the house to where our new parents couldn't see. And the look Stephen gave me then, so full of righteous indignation and pure concern, hadn't changed a bit in the twenty odd years between then and now.

"Byron," I said, settling into a seat across from him at the table.

"Byron," he confirmed. "He stopped by work this morning, asking if I'd talked to you." At my deep breath and long exhalation, Stephen said, "Don't be pissed at him. He was sweet, and really worried."

"I know he is."

"He's a good guy."

"I know."

"I think he loves you."

"I think you should stop being his PR manager."

"Tell me what happened."

I opened my mouth and closed it. Where to start? And how much to tell? One look at my brother's open, pleading features was enough to crumble the levy of half truths. If I was going to tell him anything, I was going to tell him everything.

I did.

When I'd finished, Stephen sat motionless, then went to my cabinet where I kept the liquor. He poured himself a few fingers of whiskey and returned to his seat, sipping at the drink for a minute before setting it down. "You're a real asshole, you know that?"

"I'm not the one who just poured a drink without asking if I wanted any."

"Goddamn it, stop it!" I flinched. He'd never raised his voice at me. Not ever. He seemed to also realize we were in new territory. The tension left his shoulders, and he sat back. "You could've died the other night."

"I know."

"And then what? What then, huh?" When I didn't answer, he tapped a finger on the table. "That shit you spew all the time about pointless trauma, you would've been part of it. You're so dead set on making a difference, you almost got yourself killed."

There was one person in the world who could say things like this to me, and he was saying it. I was speared by the words—my own thoughts spoken out loud by the only person I loved. Was there anything more powerful?

"I know. Maybe that's what I've always been doing. Trying to make sense of senselessness."

He studied me, maybe waiting for more. There was none. "There's these movies I watch sometimes, these shitty overwrought dramas about bad childhoods and finding the silver lining. It's always the silver lining with these writers and directors. Like a happy ending is the only ending. Like there has to be closure when most of the time there isn't. And I wonder sometimes what fucking planet these people live on." He finished his drink. Merrill appeared at his side and placed his head on Stephen's thigh. Stephen scratched his ear.

"You're right," I said.

"I know."

"No, I mean about everything."

"I know." We both smiled a little. "I love you. That's why I want you to stop. It's selfish, but I don't care." When I didn't reply, he stood and said, "I should probably go."

I followed him to the door. The rain still fell in undulating curtains. "I can't control you any more than I could control Paul," he said, looking out at the storm. I didn't know what to say so I said nothing. "Should it feel this sad to know that?"

That crushed me a little. I opened my mouth to reply, maybe to give in, but then Stephen was reaching inside his jacket and taking something out.

An iPad.

"The original was junk, but Leigh was able to transfer everything onto this spare he had. Whatever you want, it should be there."

I took the iPad and moved to hug him, but he'd already stepped away. "How much did it cost?" I asked.

He stopped at the edge of the porch. "Dinner with Leigh tomorrow night." He half smiled. Then he went down the stairs into the rain and was gone.

36

My hands shook.

I sat at the dining room table with the iPad. Its dark screen reflected my face. I didn't look like me. I wondered who I would be after seeing what was on the device. Wondered if I was already someone else.

The iPad wasn't password or ID protected. It opened up as soon as my thumb hit the home button. A solid-black background supported the standard apps in their various colors. There was a second page, and swiping revealed four added applications. A coloring-book app, a YouTube app, a game called Ruby Rove, and something named ParentVantage.

My eyes snagged on the last application. It had none of the bright, bubbly text the others shared beside it. Instead it was square with tight lettering. Serious. My finger hovered over it.

Touched it.

The screen opened to a simple uncluttered interface. The tabs and options meant nothing for a few seconds, but slowly they formed a cohesive whole, and the idea that had been floating just out of reach solidified. I sucked in a breath.

A nanny cam. The app was part of a surveillance system for parents.

In the dropdown menu a number of selections presented themselves. One was *Archived Video*. I selected it. There were seven files saved in descending order by date. The first was nearly four months ago. I hit play.

The progress wheel spun, and then the screen opened to a view of Bethany's bedroom framed by a few dark strings invading the camera at the top and bottom of the frame. Bethany appeared and dropped down to look directly into the camera. She grinned. *You're sneaky, Mr. Bubba. You were watching me this whole time and you never said anything.* And with that, the connection snapped into place. Because the camera height along with the fine strings in the view pane tracked perfectly. The strings weren't strings at all.

They were tufts of fur.

The nanny cam was hidden in the purple stuffed bear Bethany had appeared with in dozens of Kaylee's posts. The purple bear that had been taken from Andrea's room the night I'd been in the Volks' house.

A brick of dread settled in my center.

Mom doesn't think I know about the camera, Bethany was saying. *I think she watched me with it when I first came here, but she doesn't really use it anymore.* A sly grin spread across her face. *I made my own account. It was easy. Now I can make videos just like Mom does.* Her face filled up the screen and blacked it out.

The video ended. I played the next in order.

The camera bobbed and swayed, panning across the upstairs corridor of the Volks' home. Bethany was carrying the bear. She moved into Mason's doorway and paused there. Mason and Andrea sat on Mason's bed playing a card game. They spoke quietly, their voices too low to pick up. Mason said something and raised his eyebrows, and Andrea giggled, shoving him playfully. The camera jiggled as Bethany raced forward and jumped onto Mason's bed between them, letting out a shriek as she scattered the cards.

What the hell, Beth? Andrea said off-screen. The camera flipped upward, and a portion of Andrea's face was visible. *You screwed up the game!*

Sorry, Bethany said. *I wanted to play too.*

If you wanted to play you could've just asked, Mason said.

Okay. Can I play? Bethany said.

There was a pause where Andrea looked away, assumedly at Mason, who was still off-screen. A glint entered her eyes. She nodded, then lunged at Bethany, yelling, *You can play tickle torture!*

Bethany screamed with laughter. The bear rolled slightly as the three kids roughhoused on the bed. For a second they were framed there, Andrea and Mason tickling the squealing Bethany. The video ended.

Thunder boomed so loud above the house, I ducked. Merrill hunched, his tail tucking between his legs. I rubbed his muzzle, trying to soothe him. Soothe myself. The snapshot of the foster siblings' relationship looped in my head even as I saw the bruising on Mason's neck.

Andrea and Mason playing a game, happy, sharing a laugh. Bethany joining in, their connection real and palpable. So natural they might've grown up together.

The next video played.

The view opened on the Volks' bright kitchen. At the far end Kaylee and Andrea stood inches apart. *It doesn't really work if a third of the kids aren't school shopping,* Kaylee was saying. *People tune in to see all of you, not just Mason and Bethy.*

I don't want to go. I bought most of my stuff online already anyway, Andrea shot back.

Yeah, and with whose money? Kaylee said.

Justin's.

Kaylee's lips became a thin white line. *We do a lot for you, you know that? A little appreciation would go a long way.*

Andrea stared at her foster mother for another moment, then stalked away. The view shifted as Bethany moved out of Andrea's path. Then she approached Kaylee, who stood looking out the kitchen's back windows.

I'll be in your video, Mommy! Bethany said as the camera joggled.

Kaylee gave her a brief look and left the kitchen. The camera angled downward until Bethany's sock feet filled up the frame.

The video ended. The next was playing, my hand moving on its own.

Bethany's face filled the screen. She put a finger to her lips in a "shushing" gesture. *Mommy said to stay upstairs because she and Daddy were watching a grown-up movie,* Bethany whispered, an impish smile on her face. *Let's see what they're watching.* The scene changed to the stairway leading to the living room. Bethany moved slowly downward until the couch and TV came into view. Kaylee and Justin sat side by side as a movie played in the mostly dark room. After a few seconds Kaylee shifted closer to Justin, nuzzling his neck. Her hand moved toward his lap, and she said something inaudible into his ear. Justin leaned away, his attention still on the screen, and propped one leg up on the couch. Kaylee stared at the side of his head for a time before glancing toward the stairway. The camera swung away as Bethany hurried up the stairs toward her room.

The video ended.

My phone chimed a text, and Merrill whined, but I ignored them both and played the next video.

The progress wheel spun, and the screen remained dark. For a second I thought an error had occurred, but then a light snapped on, and Bethany appeared, sitting on the edge of her bed, blinking sleepily. A muffled voice came from somewhere nearby, and Bethany sat still, listening. Then she picked up the stuffed bear and made her way to her door, which was slightly open, spilling faint light in from the hall. She placed the bear at the opening, and the voices became clearer.

Justin Volk stood at the far end of the hall, leaning over something at his feet. The corridor was only half-lit, and shadows spilled everywhere. Justin said, *Nothing, do you understand?* and shifted slightly to reveal Mason sitting against the wall. The boy was gasping and holding his throat. Mason nodded and looked to his left, where something moved.

Andrea. She hovered in her own bedroom doorway, then slowly closed the door.

Justin turned away from Mason, and the camera tilted backward. The scene spun, bounced, then stilled as Bethany came into view, snapping her light off. She lay down in her bed and closed her eyes. A slant of light fell across her face, then disappeared. After a moment Bethany's eyes opened again. She stared into the camera.

The video ended.

What had I just watched? I checked the video's date confirming what I already knew. It was the aftermath of Andrea and Mason's altercation. Except Justin had been there, had been standing over Mason telling him something. Threatening him.

My head spun.

Here was the piece I'd missed. How I'd noticed Bethany's answers were delayed when I'd questioned her about the incident. How she'd seemed removed, hesitant, and yet I'd written it off as her being shy.

There were two videos left.

My mouth was dry.

I played the next in line.

Bright sunshine splashed the upstairs hallway as Bethany carried the stuffed animal out of her room. The view bounced with each of her steps until Mason's door came into view. It was slightly open, and after a second's hesitation, Bethany moved forward, pressing the bear's face to the gap.

Andrea stood with her back to the camera, arms crossed over her chest. Mason sat on his bed looking down at his lap, the bruising on his throat a deep purple. *I'm sorry,* Andrea said. When Mason didn't respond, she turned away and headed toward the door. Bethany leaped back as it swung open, and Andrea was framed there, surprise widening her eyes. *What're you doing?* she asked Bethany.

Playing, Bethany said. Andrea pushed past her, moving toward her own room. *Do you wanna play a game?* Bethany asked.

No.

How about I model for a new sketch? Lisa Martin in my class has a really pretty shirt with shiny stars and buttons. You could draw something like that for me.

Andrea spun. *Leave me alone.*

Bethany halted and Andrea went to her room, slamming the door shut. The camera panned after a beat to Bethany's face. Her brow was drawn down and tears stood in her eyes. She started to say something, then stopped.

The video ended.

A gust of wind nudged the windows, spattered them with rain. I sat watching the speckles run together and join until they snaked down the pane. My phone trilled again, but I barely heard. I was in those videos, existing in the snippets of a dead girl's attempt to emulate her mother. Seeing what she saw, but with different eyes.

My stomach flexed, and I thought I might be sick.

I played the last video.

37

The progress wheel spun so long I thought it would never load.

Then it did. The screen came to life, revealing Bethany's room. She was setting up what looked like a tea party with half a dozen other stuffed animals and plastic figurines around place settings of cups and saucers. She hummed something off-key to herself as she served imaginary tea. Eventually she focused on the camera and said, *Andrea sneaks out at night. She doesn't think anyone knows, but I do. I was going to the bathroom one night and heard her window going up, and when I looked in her room she was gone.*

Bethany served more tea and sipped some of her own. *Mom thinks Andrea's the best for her videos, but I'm going to show her she sneaks out, and then she'll want me to be in them instead.*

She hummed a little more, then stood and picked up the stuffed bear and carried it out into the hallway. Andrea's voice mingling with Kaylee's floated up the stairs. It sounded like an argument. Bethany continued on, pushing open Andrea's bedroom door and stepping inside. She moved to the futon where an accumulation of clothes and a few other stuffed animals were situated in a heap. The camera turned and faced the room. Bethany adjusted the bear, then stepped back, glancing around once as if to make sure everything was right. She left the scene, and after a minute of the empty room, the video went dark.

I blinked, thinking I'd missed something, a raging disappointment gathering that this was all there was. A precipice of wondering. But there were still several minutes of recording left. Just as I reached to scroll forward, the video resumed.

Andrea entered the room, and I realized Bethany had set the camera to only record when it sensed motion. Andrea moved a few things around on her drafting table, then walked out of frame.

The video stopped, then resumed.

It was much later. The light was gone from outside the windows, and the big trees in the backyard were only deeper shadows. Andrea entered the scene, readied for bed, and climbed beneath the covers. After a few minutes of shifting she lay still.

Another gap.

As the video played again Andrea reached toward her nightstand and picked up her phone. Texted. Then she rose and dressed in jeans and a sweatshirt. Glancing around the room once, she slid open the tall window leading to the back porch roof and climbed out, shutting the window behind her.

The video stopped. I was leaning close to the screen now, eyes aching, waiting. There was a minute left.

The video played.

Andrea's window slid up, and she appeared in the opening, climbing back inside her room carefully without a sound. She paused there, looking back out at the night, and I stared into the darkness, waiting for someone to follow her. For the person she was seeing to perhaps appear there and reveal themselves.

She shut the window.

The screen went dark. I waited, then noticed the blankness of the device was of a new definition. The battery had died.

"Oh, fuck you!" I yelled, and Merrill jerked from where he lay on the floor. I took the iPad to the kitchen counter and fumbled with the charger for a second before managing to plug it in. My hands buzzed unpleasantly like I'd slept on them and they were waking up. "Come on, come on," I said, staring at the dark screen. The startup symbol finally appeared, and at the same time my phone buzzed again. I picked it up. There were two text messages waiting, both from the same number.

> This is Beverly Harden, Natalie Winston's assistant. She received your message and is willing to video call you if you're available. Please respond soon as Ms. Winston has another appointment this afternoon.

The second message was basically the same—now or never, last chance . . .

I glanced from the booting iPad to the phone, and finally texted Natalie's assistant. By the time I'd gotten myself a glass of water and drank half of it to ease the parched feeling in my throat, the phone had lit up with an incoming FaceTime call.

Natalie was even more striking than her headshot. Her hair was dyed a dark auburn, and she wore light makeup, long mascaraed lashes highlighting pale-aquamarine eyes.

"Miss McTavish," she said, professional, direct. "Or is it Missus?"

I suffered a brief memory of Augustus Volk asking almost the same thing, then said, "Nora is fine. Thank you so much for returning my call." *I didn't really expect it* was the rest I didn't say.

"You're welcome. What can I do for you?"

"Like I mentioned in my message, I work for child services and had a few questions about your sister's foster children." Now speaking to this woman who would undoubtedly go on to make dozens of successful films and be as removed from the average person's existence as one could get, my inquiry seemed pointless. An exercise leading in a circle back to nowhere.

"I can't say I really knew them," Natalie said, confirming my thoughts. "I met them a few times over the last couple of years. I'm not usually in the area much. I travel a lot and live in LA."

"Of course. I was just wondering since it's part of a follow-up I'm doing, given the recent tragedy."

"It's a goddamn shame," Natalie said, shifting in her seat. The blunt assessment surprised me. "Such a waste. I can't believe that girl would have it in her to do something like this."

"That's partly what I'm trying to understand. I've been talking with your sister, and she wants to make sense of it too." Natalie seemed to absorb this and go somewhere else for a beat. "Did you notice anything odd in the time prior to the crash?" I said.

"Like?"

"Anything Kaylee or Justin mentioned." I hesitated, then surged forward. "There's a concern Justin was abusing prescription drugs."

"You're kidding."

"It hasn't been confirmed, but—"

"Seems unlike him." She appeared to gauge me, then added, "Always thought women were his addiction."

"What do you mean?"

"Nothing, forget it. It's neither here nor there, now Kaylee's gone through enough."

"You think he was having an affair?"

"No, I didn't say that. He just always seemed like the type. The few times I met him he gave off that vibe. Chatted me up, checked me out. Felt like if I'd shown even a shred of interest, he would've been all over it." I thought of Justin's father nudging my foot with his own within minutes of meeting me. Maybe the apple hadn't tumbled very far from the creepy old tree. "But that's just me. Please don't mention it to Kaylee. She'd probably say that I think all the men I meet want to fuck me." She grimaced. "Sorry. We don't have the best relationship. It's one of those things—you don't know how it happened, but you just don't talk anymore. There's nothing to say to each other even though you're related."

"Family is complicated," I offered.

She made a sound that could've been an agreement and glanced off-screen. "I'm really sorry to be so brief, but if you don't have anything else I can help with, I've got to be across town in an hour . . ."

"No, I appreciate your time."

"If you see Kaylee, tell her I hope she's feeling better. I sent a message and a bouquet of flowers but didn't hear back." She faded again, those pale-green eyes going somewhere else. "It's a miracle she survived. Twice in five years."

I was about to say goodbye but stopped cold. "What do you mean, 'twice in five years'?"

Natalie came back from wherever she'd gone. "Her car accident."

"I wasn't aware of an accident."

"It was right before she met Justin. Before things turned around for her. She lost control of her car and crashed. An accident." Natalie paused. "At least that's what it was listed as."

"I don't understand."

"It's stupid. Nothing."

"No, I'd like to hear."

She looked away again, maybe to check the clock, maybe to work herself up to what she was about to say. "Kaylee was in a bad place for a long time. She couldn't get over what happened with our parents. She thought they were perfect, that everything in our lives was perfect. When it all came crashing down, it really messed her up. She called me a couple days before the accident, and it sounded like she was drunk or something. She was talking gibberish. Saying stuff about how Dad didn't really kill himself and how maybe someone poisoned Mom. It was pure deflection and delusion. She couldn't get over it. She said"—I waited, heart banging against my breastbone—"that she didn't want to live anymore. I tried talking to her but she hung up. I put in a call with her school's counselor but didn't hear back. The next thing I knew she was in the hospital. She was okay, but that's why she couldn't have kids of her own. Unbelievable it wasn't worse since she wasn't wearing her seat belt."

I tried to find my voice and failed for a moment. "You think she crashed her car on purpose?"

Natalie stared at me through the phone. "I don't see how it wasn't since she went off the highway at the exact same place our mother had her accident."

———

The floor wasn't steady anymore. Wasn't still. Everything around me shifted and swam, like reality itself would suddenly give way and reveal something else behind it. Something darkly lit and waiting to be seen.

There was a smear of liquor in Stephen's glass. I poured a healthy splash on top. Downed it. The burn in my throat and stomach brought me back. Tethered me so I wouldn't float away. The conversation with Natalie was an echo chamber, my thoughts bouncing within it. Slowly I moved to the iPad and hit the home button. Ten percent battery. Good enough.

Back at the table I reopened ParentVantage and found the final video, scrolling to the place where I'd left off. Andrea had just reentered her room after sneaking out. She stood there in the faint wash of light. My finger hovered. Fell.

The video played.

Andrea shut the window and stepped away from it, beginning to get ready for bed again. No one had followed her inside. Another few seconds ticked by before she startled, looking past the camera's far frame, seeing something out of view. For a beat she was frozen, then she moved across the room and reached for something.

For someone.

There was somebody else there with her in the dark. Andrea stepped close to them, leaned into their arms. Kissed them.

They stayed that way for a moment, framed there in the low light, embracing like the lovers they were.

The video ended.

38

Taylor wasn't answering her phone.

It rang, and rang, and rang. Her voice mail wasn't personalized, just a recording that the party I was trying to reach was unavailable. I didn't leave a message. I called again.

No answer.

The knowledge in my head was volcanic. Searing everything else away. I needed to get it out, needed to confirm what I already knew. Needed to do something.

Do what?

What could I do exactly with what I knew? That got me pacing. Merrill whined briefly and retreated to the living room as if I were making him nervous. I probably was, but I couldn't stop moving. The storm was inside me now, churning and tearing things apart, rearranging them into a new picture that was hard to accept. Hard to believe.

The phone rang. Detective Tern.

My jaw worked for a second, priming the words to come, but even then it sounded crazy, unhinged. And what proof did I have?

"Nora?" Tern said quickly, "Glad I caught you. Do you know an Evan Baker?"

Of all the things I thought she'd say, I hadn't expected that. "Yes. I mean, I've met him."

"We found his car abandoned a mile from the park where you were attacked. He hasn't been to work the last two days. Do you have any reason to think he'd want to hurt you?"

Yes. I almost blurted it out. *Yes, now that I've seen what's on that iPad, yes, I think he definitely would.* "I'm not sure," was what I told her.

"Given no one's seen him and with his vehicle still parked where it is, I'd say he didn't survive the fall into the river. If something turns up I'll call you, and we'll need to do another interview, at the station." She said the last like it was a formality, but it didn't feel so. It felt like a promise. A threat. Then she was saying goodbye and was gone before I could add anything else. Not that I was going to.

Something spurred by Tern's call returned to me then. Something about the hospital where Kaylee had been treated. The first day I'd visited her after the crash. What was it? Something small, innocuous.

I moved to the windows and looked out at the falling rain, not seeing it. For a second the memory tried slipping away, then it returned and it was like I was reliving it.

Standing at the nurse's station, asking what room Kaylee was in. Turning and running into someone—a man who kept going without looking back. How he moved, stalking forward with purpose. The same way my attacker had stridden across the parking lot in the dark. Of course.

Evan Baker.

He'd been at the hospital visiting his sister just before I'd seen her. Kaylee had even said his name when I'd appeared at her door. *Ev?* Yet both had denied having anything to do with one another for years.

Now I knew why.

My hands shook as I made to pour a fresh drink but stopped. Couldn't be sloppy for this, whatever this was. I needed a clear mind to make sense of everything, to understand, if something like this could be understood.

Somehow I knew Taylor would answer this time when I called. So it was no surprise that on the third ring she picked up and asked breathlessly who the hell it was.

"It's Nora McTavish."

"What do you want?" There was an edge to her voice. Not quite panic, but something close. She'd been crying.

I took a breath. "It was Justin Volk. Andrea was seeing her foster father."

Dead silence. Crypt-like. The sound of secrets finally revealing themselves. "I don't know what you're—"

"Cut the shit, Taylor. I know. They were sleeping together. Maybe even before she turned eighteen. I know." Taylor breathed out a half sob, the relinquishing of a weight. "Now tell me what you know." I let her work the courage up to do so. Eventually she did.

"I have no idea when it started. Just that she was different one day. Not so angry. She said she'd met someone and she'd introduce me soon. I didn't know, you have to believe me, I didn't know who it was." Taylor inhaled a shaky breath. "She started talking about the future, which was totally not like her. She talked about graduating and opening a clothing company with a store and everything. I thought she was crazy. But she was so sure. She talked like it was already a reality. I didn't know why until she finally told me."

Justin Volk. His money. His promises. I could see how it had played out—the younger woman living under his roof, vulnerable and hoping for a better future. It was only a matter of time.

"I told her she was crazy and it was gross she was fucking her foster father, but she said he was just a guy. It didn't matter who he was, only that he cared about her. That he loved her. She said he was going to leave his wife," Taylor was saying. "That she was driving him insane with the perfect-family influencer bullshit. Andrea said he wanted kids of his own, and Kaylee couldn't give him any." She sniffled. "But Andrea could."

Dominoes, lined up perfectly. Only needing that first push. Strangely enough the push had been a little girl's need to be important and included. Bethany had felt overshadowed by Andrea's presence and conflict in Kaylee's videos. So she'd done what was only natural to a nine-year-old—she'd tried to make herself seen again. By doing so she'd unwittingly exposed something not meant to be seen. And the fight. She'd only caught the tail end of the conflict, but I could imagine what preceded it. Could see Mason stumbling upon Andrea and Justin together, could see Justin reacting, grasping Mason's throat, threatening him not to say anything—the cover story of a fight between Andrea and Mason. And since they were minors the only repercussion would be a visit from child services and the minimum court requirements going forward.

Until Bethany showed Kaylee what was on her iPad.

I could see that moment too. Could see Kaylee watching the final video with a growing horror until her worst fears became reality. The picture of her perfect family shattered, the picture she'd redrawn after losing it all as a child. I could see the whiteness of her knuckles as she gripped the iPad before flinging it away. Saw it hit the bedroom wall and fall behind the dresser where it lay until I found it. And I could see the brokenness in Kaylee's eyes change and become something else.

A reckoning. A plan.

"I didn't say anything because what did it matter?" Taylor said, bringing me back. "They were all dead. I mean, it doesn't change anything."

It did. It changed everything. Of course she didn't know that, and I wasn't about to tell her. "Don't worry, you're not in trouble," I said.

Taylor huffed a laugh and sniffled again. "Maybe I am. Maybe I'm going crazy."

For a second I thought she was referring to keeping Andrea's secret after everything that had happened. Then I recalled how anxious she'd sounded answering the phone. "What's wrong, Taylor?"

She exhaled, long and slow. A humming silence. "Someone broke into my house while I was at work. I don't know where my dad is, but he's gonna kill me when he gets home."

"Why?"

"Because they stole one of his guns. It's not on the table anymore. And—" Her voice strangled as she started to cry again.

I waited, feeling something akin to sitting on my board in the ocean and knowing a large wave was building somewhere farther out, coming closer. Growing. "What?" I asked quietly. "What is it?"

"Andrea," she finally blurted out, crying harder now. "I saw whoever broke in running away from the house, and—and it looked like Andrea."

39

The subconscious is a serious person with a clipboard and a list.

It observes and checks boxes, scribbles little notes in the margins of our thoughts. It watches and catalogs and hopes the person in which it resides can't possibly be as dense as they seem. And yet it is unsurprised as we stumble through mistake after mistake, oblivious to its cues.

For a while I wasn't able to do anything but sit at the table—thoughts and images cascading through my head in an avalanche of conclusions.

The Volks' neighbors calling in a prowler near the home.

The bloody bandages in the Volks' upstairs bathroom.

The pungent scent of soap and shampoo in Andrea's room.

The trail of clothing, scattered on her floor as if someone had recently been there.

Standing outside the house with the feeling of being watched.

There were a million other explanations for everything, all of them more reasonable and likelier than the other notion trying to loom over me, its shadow cloistering, smothering.

And yet . . .

Byron didn't answer his phone. I hadn't expected him to. I paced as I left a voice mail asking him to call me. Please. It was important. I sent a text saying the same thing. While waiting I pulled up Kaylee's channel on YouTube. Her livestream was scheduled to begin in twenty minutes. I scrolled back through her videos, screenshots of her dead family streaming past in quick succession until one in particular caught my eye.

Beach Day! The caption beneath the post exclaimed. I hit play and watched the Volks pack for an excursion to the shore. The kids in their beach attire. The family climbing in their van, all smiles. I scrolled ahead to their arrival and inched forward by seconds, searching for identifying landmarks. I'd surfed dozens of spots over the years and was familiar with a lot of beaches, but there were so many more I hadn't been to.

"Come on, come on," I breathed. Kaylee spread a blanket out on a perfect section of sand while Bethany cartwheeled nearby. Justin grinned, taking off his shirt to reveal a gym-sculpted torso. Mason opened a book and disappeared behind the cover. Andrea preened in a bikini before wading through ankle-deep waves rushing ashore.

There. The rocks on the far right of the frame. They were tumbled together in a rough semblance of an animal stretching its neck out toward the water.

Horsehead Beach.

There was still time.

After a brief hesitation I dialed Kaylee's number. It went directly to voice mail. She'd shut it off for the livestream, probably using a separate phone for all her YouTube posts. I swore loudly, and Merrill padded into the room, ears pricked.

It was insane, this conclusion I'd jumped to. Wildly crazy. But everything seemed to support it, aligning into an arrow pointing at one possibility.

I had to go.

In the car, backing quickly out the drive, my phone rang. Byron.

"What's going on? Are you all right?" he asked. A car swung around me as I backed in front of it onto the street, its horn shrill and blasting as I stomped the brakes. "What was that?"

"You said Andrea's body was in rough shape. Did they have to use dental records for the ID?" I asked, throwing the car into gear. My foot punched the gas, and I was hurtling through the neighborhood, a speed bump rattling everything in the car.

"What?"

"Dental records to identify her body—did they need them to make sure it was her?" There was dead silence on the other end. It was all I needed to know for sure.

"How did you know?" Byron sounded dazed.

"It wasn't her, was it?"

"No. There was another girl who went missing a couple of weeks back who fit Andrea's description. Why are you asking? What's going on?"

The landscape flashed past as I formed what to say next. "She's still alive. Andrea survived the crash."

"What are you talking about?"

"She made it through somehow, just like Kaylee. Must've drifted in the storm and made it to shore. She was staying at the Volks' for the last week. Biding her time."

"Listen, I know you've been stressed lately, and I haven't been helping by telling you about the case—"

"She must've seen Kaylee survived too," I said, almost to myself. Some of the pieces were still falling into place. "That's why she didn't notify anyone. She saw that Kaylee was blaming her for the crash, but she didn't do it. Andrea didn't crash the plane." I took a breath. "Kaylee did."

Quiet again from his end. Then, "I don't know what you're talking about, but it sounds like you're driving. Tell me where you are, and I'll come to you."

"Horsehead Beach. Kaylee's livestreaming a memorial there."

"That's where you are?"

"It's where I'm going."

"Why?"

I sucked in a breath, narrowly avoiding a garbage truck lumbering out of a side street before blasting past it.

"Because Andrea's going to kill Kaylee."

40

Horsehead Beach was fifteen minutes north of the city. I could see why Kaylee had chosen it for family outings.

The drive was one thing—most people preferred the half dozen beaches within walking distance of downtown—but the aesthetics of Horsehead were also a factor. It wasn't a long beach, and parts were rocky. The shore dropped off quickly to deep water, and several boulders lay just beneath the waves, exposing themselves at low tide but submerging to form unseen hazards to swimmers and surfers whenever the water was up. Not a typically frequented beach, in other words. A place where an influencer could bring their family without too much worry of being recognized.

The rain hadn't stopped on the drive over. If anything, it came down harder. The steady thrum of the windshield wipers was a rhythm section for my thoughts—an orchestra of reckoning drawing my nerves tighter with each passing mile.

Evan Baker. The missing link in all this. Kaylee must have called on her little brother after discovering her life was about to come apart at the seams. He was her contact for the drugs she'd needed to execute her plan, to dose Justin enough so he couldn't fight back once they were in the air. How much had she offered Evan for the drugs? How much had it taken for him to break the conditions of his parole? And how much had she promised him to retrieve the only incriminating evidence from her house while she'd been in the hospital? How much to find the purple bear with its camera hidden inside, and the iPad?

Instead it had cost him his life.

I inhaled a shaky breath. How? How could Kaylee have done it all? Spent days planning out the end to her family, her own death? But the answer came just as quickly. She'd already endured this once before—a rupture of the perfect life, of family falling apart so badly it seemed nothing would ever be right again. And she hadn't been willing to go through it a second time, wouldn't watch her husband leave her, not only for a younger woman, but for their own foster daughter as well. The scandalous betrayal would've been too much, considering Kaylee's public persona. And what about Bethany and Mason? Had she considered them? Their futures and possibilities? I guessed she'd reasoned she was sparing them the hurt and shame that would come in the inevitable aftermath. The same pain she'd barely survived in her youth.

Except this time there would be no suffering because there would be no one left alive.

The exit for the beach appeared, and I swung the car into it, rain sluicing up from the tires in fans of silver. The road followed the top of a low cliff above the beach, and after a second the shoreline came into view.

There was a crowd on the sand. Not too large, but not small either. Probably subscribers to Kaylee's channel who had done the same detective work I had and deduced the memorial's location. I scanned the bodies, still a clump of humanity rather than individuals, and wondered if Andrea was already there among them.

Andrea. A survivor if there ever was one. She hadn't asked to be beaten by her father or be run through the ringer of the child welfare system. Hadn't asked to be placed with the Volks. And I was sure she hadn't intended to fall for Justin. Hadn't planned on putting her faith in him, in his promises of what she could have if they were together, of the life she never dreamed was possible for someone like her. I thought of Andrea and Mason and Bethany on Mason's bed. The three kids who had endured what so many other people would never be able to fathom. Thought of their laughter as they tickled Bethany.

Andrea had loved them too.

There'd been no blue or red flashing lights in my rearview on the drive, and when I shut the car off in the parking lot and stepped into the storm, there were no sirens either. Byron had said he'd be here, that he'd hurry. But would he? Did he believe me? Or had I burned a few too many bridges with him, acted a little too unstable?

Time would tell.

A makeshift cordon had been set up near the water's edge, a few flimsy stands holding a ribbon to keep people back. Kaylee stood on the other side of the barrier, holding a phone. She was dressed in a white slicker with the hood back. Her hair streamed rain. It was like ice water in the face to see her now. To know what she'd done. How she'd sent Evan to my home and desecrated my sanctuary. To know how she'd tried manipulating me. She hadn't planned on surviving the plane crash but had quickly realized her slate was blank again. She'd been rejuvenated by the sympathy that came with her continuing life.

Kaylee smiled at someone near the front of the small crowd and put a hand over her heart. Her lips formed the words *thank you.*

With the rain there were slickers. Hooded slickers hiding people's faces. Umbrellas shielding them from view. There were more people here than I'd originally thought. Too many to wind through and identify quickly.

I made my way along the right side of the crowd until I could cut in front of it. Kaylee's security was there, a black baseball cap pulled down tight and a windbreaker cinched at his waist. He was eyeing the crowd, one hand resting lightly on his Taser, cosplaying secret service. When he spotted my approach and noticed I wasn't slowing down, he turned and headed me off.

"Ma'am, please step back," he said as I leaned around him.

"Kaylee! It's Nora." She was still talking with the person who had given her condolences or a compliment. There were four large wreaths near her feet. She didn't look my way. "Kaylee!" She turned her head, and we locked eyes.

She knew I knew.

I don't know how. It must've been something, some visible change or difference in me. The knowledge of what she'd done written on my face. How did you hide the fact you knew someone was a monster? She raised her chin slightly, a coolness entering her gaze. Then she was glancing away, smiling again at something someone else had said.

"Ma'am, step back. Now." Mr. Security gripped my shoulder with a powerful hand and steered me toward the back of the crowd.

"Her life's in danger," I told him. A few heads turned our way as we passed, curiosity at the spectacle—an unhinged follower being shown the door.

"Thank you for your concern," he said, continuing to ferry me along.

"Do you not remember me?" I asked as he let me go. "I came to the hotel room."

"You'll have to discuss this with Mrs. Volk at a later time," he said, tapping his Taser, then returning to his post at the cordon.

Kaylee was saying something muted by the rain. Something about thanking everyone for being here. The rest was lost as people pressed forward, getting a closer look at the grieving woman, the miraculous survivor. I wondered then what she was thinking, if she was thrown off by my appearance, our unspoken understanding. Was she worried, or was she all-consumed by the presence of the crowd, the ones who would brave a storm for her, to witness her sorrow in real time? Her family was gone, but she had these people.

I threaded my way through the mass, skirting a cluster too tight to penetrate, searching faces shadowed by hoods. I pictured Andrea's height and build, tried matching them to any of the figures in the throng. I angled around each potential until their faces appeared. All the while Kaylee kept talking.

"It really means a lot," she was saying now. "It's been so hard, but all your support and outpouring of love has gotten me this far." Kaylee paused, and I continued to weave through the crowd. "Seeing the ocean, being in the rain, it's so much like that day. It's almost like fate." She knelt and gathered one of the wreaths, held it to her chest awkwardly using her casted arm. There were tears or raindrops on her cheeks. She had her eyes closed. "It's been a week but feels like years since I saw them."

I slowed in my search and gave her my full attention. Full ire. I hoped she could feel it. For a second I saw myself running at her, hands out in claws—felt them around her neck. Squeezing.

Kaylee opened her eyes. "They're close. I can feel them." She smiled and bit back a sob as there was a rumble of comforting sounds and agreements from the crowd. *They sure are. They'll never leave you. They're in your heart.*

At the far side of the gathering I paused, looking back the way I'd come. Scanning as many faces as I could. Was she here? Waiting? Watching?

Or was I wrong?

There was a chance—more than a chance really—that I was. All the signs could've been other things completely. Mistaken for importance when they were happenstance.

Somewhere in the distance a siren swelled.

Still holding the phone, Kaylee set the first wreath on the water. It bobbed and dipped in the waves but almost immediately started floating out to deeper water. The crowd watched it. I watched them. Kaylee set the next and the next to float, saying something low—only for her, the departed, and those watching online. The last wreath she held longer, staring down at it as if seeing it for the first time. It was apparent whose wreath it was. Andrea's. Those watching understood too. There were a few whispers loud enough to hear. "Doesn't deserve it . . . Murderer . . . Crazy bitch." I gazed around at those who had spoken. If they only knew what I did. What I *thought* I did. The siren was closer.

Kaylee set the last wreath on the water and it swayed, washing back once in a slosh of foam before drawing out toward the shapes of the other wreaths already growing smaller and harder to find in the waves. Kaylee stood that way, framed there in the rain against the backdrop of ocean. Alone. Then she turned and addressed the phone in her hand as well as everyone present.

"They're at peace now. I hope someday I can be too." Her face crumpled, but she soldiered on. "I'd like a moment of silence now. Please think of those who have left us, and be thankful for the ones still here."

Kaylee lowered her head. The crowd followed suit.

I searched the sea of downturned faces for one looking forward but saw none. The surety that had gripped me an hour ago eroded. It was no longer ironclad but rusting and flaking away with each passing second. I'd drawn the wrong conclusions somehow, skewed the picture.

What was I doing here?

This was me. Making this whole thing about myself. Seeing myself in these kids, seeing Paul. Seeing my own pain and past etched in every family to the point of delusion.

None of this is real.

Stephen would be vindicated. He'd warned me out of love. Byron too. And now here I was, soaking with rain and my own insecurities. My own mistakes.

I made my way back through the crowd, a straight line toward the parking lot. I'd intercept the police car making all the noise that was coming closer and closer. Hopefully it was Byron. I'd explain what happened. False alarm. Maybe everything would eventually become clear, all the suspicions revealing themselves for the innocuous things they were.

I was so deep in thought I almost didn't notice when someone passed me moving in the opposite direction.

41

They were rain-slickered. Hooded. Petite. Not abiding the moment of silence.

I stopped and they kept moving. Navigating around silently swaying people, mourning avatars they'd never known.

"Andrea," I said. They kept going. Hadn't heard me. I followed.

First being careful, then hurrying, bumping into others and jostling exclamations from them. I lost sight of them for a beat, then they appeared almost at the head of the masses. Right in front of Kaylee.

I pushed and shoved, throwing my shoulder into backs and sides, stepping on toes.

A hand grabbed my shoulder, and I spun away.

They were almost there, stepping between the last row at the front. I jagged to the left, finding an open lane, hurried the last dozen steps, and broke into the open.

They stepped into the gap between the onlookers and the cordon at the same time, and things became suspended.

They reached up and brushed back their hood, letting the rain stream down through their blonde hair.

Andrea.

There were dark circles beneath her eyes. A fading bruise colored the side of her jaw. Her lips had split and were healing. But it was undoubtedly her.

She moved fluidly, not taking her eyes off Kaylee, who still had her head lowered, hadn't noticed the minor commotion I'd caused, didn't see who had appeared. Her lips moved silently.

Andrea pulled something from her pocket and raised her arm.

A gun.

It was dark and beaded with moisture. A deadly statement in her fist.

Someone shouted. People staggered back, the crowd parting like a school of fish around a shark. Kaylee finally looked up.

And saw.

Her arm went limp, dropping her phone to her side, then releasing it onto the sand. Her mouth opened weakly, eyes wide and staring. Unblinking.

Andrea took another step forward, stopping at the cordon. The security guard and I were still suspended. He got moving first.

He took two steps toward Andrea, yanking blindly at his Taser without releasing it from the holster. He was saying something, but a stutter broke his commands into meaningless syllables. Rain sprayed from his lips. Andrea angled the gun toward him as he neared, and his hands shot up. He reversed the way he'd come, getting himself out of the stare of the gun's eye.

Andrea shifted, recentering the pistol on Kaylee. Then I was there, not recalling moving, just arriving a few paces to Andrea's left and speaking her name.

She glanced my way, arm twitching as if to ward me off as well before seeing who I was. A hint of recognition passed over her face, then she focused on Kaylee again.

"Andrea, listen to me, please," I said, hands open and extended toward her. I had no idea what to say, what to do. "We can talk." Kaylee hadn't moved since dropping the phone. Her eyes shot from Andrea to me, back to Andrea. I licked my lips. *Come on, come on, come on. Do something.* "I know, Andrea. I know what happened."

Andrea stared ahead, rain beading and running in rivulets down the side of her face.

The gun shook.

I took a step closer, feeling like I stood on the edge of a chasm. "I know," I repeated, hoping she'd believe. Hoping she'd understand I was an ally, that I would back up her claims of innocence. "Things can still be okay," I said, throat so dry my voice cracked. "Put the gun down, and we'll talk. Just you and me."

The siren was louder, almost to the beach's turnoff. Within seconds the cruiser would appear and everything would change again.

Andrea's lips curled back from her teeth. Her arm shook harder.

"It's not over," I said. "You're alive. It's not over."

The police cruiser crested the rise above the beach and descended to the parking lot, lights flashing, siren hiccupping once, then going silent. Andrea didn't seem to notice. She was hyperfocused on Kaylee, the snarl still twisting her mouth. I was close enough to see her finger going white on the trigger.

She was going to do it.

"Your clothes," I said, not thinking. Grabbing the first thing flying into my mind and thrusting it at her. "Your designs are beautiful, Andrea." A beat. No gunshot. Her eyes flicked to me and away. "They're really striking. Maybe no one's told you, but you're very talented. You are." A softening in her shoulders, her posture. Was I imagining it? Or was this working?

A figure moved across the parking lot toward us in my periphery, hand on their duty belt. *Stay back. Wait, please just wait, and it will be okay. I can fix this.*

"I saw your store too. Parish Unlimited. It's lovely." I waited, saw the gun drop maybe an inch, and pressed on. "It's still possible. Everything is. I promise."

Those moments when you know things will never be the same.

I saw my mother walking down to the curb with a suitcase in one hand and never looking back.

I saw the closet door opening and Paul's body, shrunken in his clothes.

I saw my father's writing on the walls, the news clips about him others tried so hard to shield us from.

Saw all the kids who had made it and the ones who hadn't, their futures spooling out or cut short.

I saw Andrea fighting for her own.

Slowly she lowered her arm.

The aching coil in my chest loosened enough to breathe. The crowd murmured, keeping their distance. When I looked toward the cop who had arrived, it was Byron. He had his gun drawn, but it was pointed at the ground, and he was speaking low into the radio on his shoulder. We shared a look. It was going to be okay.

Kaylee took a step forward. "Andrea—"

Andrea raised the gun and shot her.

The sound cracked flatly through the rain and echoed off the rocks.

People screamed, scattering in every direction.

A black hole appeared on the chest of Kaylee's white slicker. Her mouth opened wide, eyes flooding with shock. Disbelief. She stayed frozen that way for a long second, then staggered back, feet tangling on themselves, the strength going out of her legs.

She tipped backward into the tide.

Andrea watched Kaylee fall, then brought the gun to her head.

"No!" I yelled, reaching for her, extending a hand for her to grab, something to hold on to.

She pulled the trigger.

42

One Year Later

"Find a spot and go, Merrill. We're both getting old here."

He threw a look over one shoulder that seemed to say, *Human, I'm trying. Can't you see? But the smells. The smells are so good this time of year.* Couldn't argue with him there.

It was late fall, almost winter. The cusp behind us at least two weeks. There was crispness in the air every morning now, and the leaves had changed and were falling off in swaths. When the wind came up, it was like standing in a hurricane of color.

We were in the backyard, Merrill sniffing along the border of the property, me standing and spinning my keys around my finger. We were leaving late. Not that we were really on a schedule, but I wanted to get going in any case. I was excited. I hadn't seen Julia or Sam in so long, and I knew Sam was aching to introduce his new puppy to Merrill. He had named the little shepherd-lab mix Sam. Maybe it was a kid's thinking—odd in a way that made total sense when you thought about it. Since Sam had a new name, a new identity, he'd given his old one to his puppy. Sam now went by Arnold (he had a thing for Schwarzenegger movies, don't ask me) and Julia was Shannon—a namesake she'd adopted from a distant aunt on her mother's side who had once given her a flower at a wedding.

I checked the time. It would be around a sixteen-hour drive to get to their place, a little town in another state where no one knew them and no one knew their history, knew what they were running from. There was only one other person in the world who knew their real identities, where they lived, and I saw her in the mirror every morning.

Merrill finally peed on a small pine tree, looking at me as he went in that embarrassed and pleading way dogs have. Then he followed me up the hill toward the driveway where the car waited, fully packed and gassed. In the passenger seat a sheaf of papers lay. I'd debated bringing them but knew Julia/Shannon would want to read them herself. Frank's sentencing had been months ago, but already his lawyer had filed an appeal, and he was up for a parole hearing in less than a year. In the interim I'd appeared on Julia's behalf at all the court proceedings, the ink on my shiny new family-advocate certifications barely dry.

Byron had urged me not to quit child services, especially before the state board reviewed the formal complaint. He said it would easily get dismissed since no one would hold me accountable for the accusations of a man who had targeted and assaulted me shortly after. Evan Baker's body had been found tangled in a deadfall six miles downriver from the park by a group of hikers the day after Horsehead Beach. By then the media frenzy was at its height, and I'd been relegated to my house, stuck alone with my thoughts and too much wine.

Byron had probably been right, but my heart wasn't in the job anymore. Hadn't been for some time if I were honest with myself. Making a difference had always been why I'd gotten up day after day and pushed papers, took stands, took kids from bad places. But after what happened on the beach, the fire had gone out to some extent. If I were really honest, the flames had been snuffed completely for a time. And those months were a dark place I tended not to dwell on. Sara had helped me then; she'd brought food, stayed the night, and we'd talked. Really talked. During one visit she told me something I'll never forget.

Everyone has something to fight for. But not everyone has someone to fight for them.

When you're given the truth, you don't throw it away.

Shortly thereafter I decided if I was going to continue to fight, I would do it on my own terms. Thus the family-advocate certification and the little office space I kept downtown not so far from where my father had doled out death. Being there and doing as much good as possible felt like a balancing of sorts. A stacking on one pan of the cosmic scale. Whether that was true or not wasn't so important. It felt right to me.

"Up," I coaxed needlessly as Merrill leaped into the back of the car. He faced me, grinning, wagging his tail. He knew we were going somewhere special. Dogs know so much more than we give them credit for. I scratched his ears and got into the front seat, sitting there in the quiet for a moment, thinking, while more leaves cascaded from the trees.

Justin Volk's body had been found a few weeks after Evan Baker's. It had washed in a quick car ride south from Horsehead Beach. DNA testing had been the only viable confirmation tool at that point. There'd been no way to tell if any drugs had been present in his system at the time of the crash. I'd checked. At that juncture my and Byron's relationship had been one of cool professionalism akin to a body in the morgue. We communicated while standing over it, moving around it in a clinically detached way until it could be rolled into the dark with the door closed behind it. We worked through those weeks of tumult, then drifted apart. We talked seldomly, only when crossing paths in court. He was seeing a nurse named Cindy and seemed happy. I was glad.

During the weeks sequestered at home, with Stephen's occasional company and too much alcohol, I'd debated going public with the story no one else was aware of. The story of a girl who had been seduced by an older man in a position of power, whose hidden dreams had finally won out over her cynicism and whose shattered hope had finally driven her to do what she'd done. Andrea's funeral had been a circus of cameras and questions. I'd attended in as much disguise as I could muster, but several intrepid reporters saw through it and harangued me as a cold rain fell. Augustus Volk made an appearance, which turned into spectacle when he spat on Andrea's coffin and nearly fell into her open grave. The investment broker was hauled away amid a tirade of drunken aspersions. He sold his business in the following months, lighting out for a sunny island somewhere in the South Pacific not long after.

In the end both Stephen and Byron had convinced me to keep the evidence of Kaylee's guilt under wraps simply because in the end it wasn't evidence at all. It was hearsay and accusations built on speculation at best. The truth is only as good as the proof backing it up. Without that, it's soft. Flexible. Malleable. You can bend it into shapes unrecognizable if there is nothing to hold it steady.

I hated Kaylee. That was the truth.

Hated her and understood how broken she was inside to do what she did. Some days it took all my will not to scream when I thought of her. Took everything not to tell a journalist what I knew, to broadcast everything, because I wanted to right things as best I could. I hadn't saved Bethany, or Mason, or Andrea, and the least I could do was tell the truth. But then Stephen would remind me how my possession of Bethany's iPad and the nanny cam videos would complicate things in legal ways. Questions would have to be asked, and most answers wouldn't prevent charges from being brought against me.

And what did it matter when everyone who could corroborate my story was dead?

I reached for the ignition but paused again, returning briefly to the twisted labyrinth I'd navigated the year before. The unfathomable depths inside people.

There are no words for what we do to each other. No words for what we are. Human beings are the strongest and weakest part of the world. And when they break, they shatter everything around them.

A flicker of something brought me back to the present. Paul had come to me less and less over the last year. But he was there now on the front porch, only a suggestion of a boy, no familiar definition. I watched him even as he faded and wondered if there would be a day when I'd wake up and not think of him. I didn't know. Maybe. But it wasn't today.

As I started the car and put it into gear, my phone chimed. A subscriber notification. One of two dozen or so I'd received in the last year. For now I would keep a close watch on the developments, and if my instincts told me to act, I would. Legal repercussions be damned.

I flicked the notification away, yet another reminder the world wasn't fair, and you had to keep going even when you wanted to stop. I'd keep focusing on what I could change, who I could help.

Because we're all to blame.

Especially if we give up.

Update and special announcement!!! | Kaylee Baker

900,578 views * Nov 2, 2023

Kaylee Baker (Kaylee's Journey)

5.7M subscribers

AN UPDATE AND SPECIAL ANNOUNCEMENT!!! Thank you all for checking in and hitting that like and subscribe button!

Video Plays

Kaylee stands in bright sunlight. A playground is blurred in the background. Her face is thinner, the angles sharpened, but her smile fills up the lens.

KAYLEE

Hi, everyone! Thanks so much for tuning in. It is a gorgeous fall day with that rare sunshine we all love so much, so we decided to venture to the park.

The shot swings away and pans across the sun-drenched park with rolling hills and old-growth trees partially bare of their bright leaves. Kaylee's face returns to the frame.

KAYLEE

Beautiful, right?

(she pauses)

Things like this, these moments of pure beauty, they mean so much more to me now after what I've gone through. The last year has truly been the hardest of my life. The loss of my family along with the attack I suffered, it was . . . something I never thought I'd survive.

She blinks away tears and fans her eyes with one hand.

KAYLEE

Gahh! I told myself I wouldn't cry again this time. There's been enough tears. But today these tears are ones of joy because I have some unbelievable news.

Kaylee motions for someone off-screen.

KAYLEE

Come here.

DEXTER CALLOWAY, thirties, bright-blue eyes, blond goatee, enters the frame, and Kaylee kisses his cheek. He grins and waves at the camera.

KAYLEE

Now, you all know this guy. Dex saved my life. Literally. After spending months in intensive care with the doctors telling me I'd never walk again, Dex entered my life as my physical therapist. I *hated* him at first!

The couple share a laugh.

KAYLEE

He was so tough, but there was love in everything he did. Love in his voice as he encouraged me. Love in his constant and unwavering supervision. And love in his hands as he steadied me while I took my first steps. And that love grew between us until it was something neither of us could deny.

They gaze at one another for a beat.

KAYLEE

So it is with pure joy we're able to announce today that we'll be getting married next spring!

Kaylee holds up her left hand, displaying a large flashing diamond ring.

KAYLEE

(biting her lip)

I can't tell you all how happy I am right now. Dex is the best thing that's ever happened to me, and I can't wait to continue our lives together.

Kaylee and Dexter hold one another close, both looking into the camera.

KAYLEE

And as an added bonus, if you're a premium subscriber to my channel, you can access Dex's proposal to me at the link below! He recorded it all, the sly devil!

Leaves flutter down in the background as the wind gusts. The sun slides behind a cloud. The scene darkens.

KAYLEE

Now I know what you're all wondering—how did two other very special people take the news? Well, that's the second surprise we have for you today. We're going to tell Dex's daughters right now as you watch and get their reaction. Call them over, honey.

Dex turns and faces a jungle gym in the distance where two girls are playing.

DEX

Haley! Blythe! Come over here for a second!

The two girls scamper down off the equipment and come running, half flying out from beneath their wool hats. One of them carries a small teddy bear.

The view holds on them, then the camera turns, and Kaylee's face fills up the screen once again. She stares into the lens.

Her smile falters for a beat, then slowly returns.

ACKNOWLEDGMENTS

Eternal thanks to my family—I wouldn't be able to do any of this without you. Thanks as always to my agent, Laura Rennert—your unwavering support is such a blessing. Thanks to my editor, Liz Pearsons, for going to bat for me and having faith in my words. Thanks to Jacque Ben Zekry and Blake Crouch; I wouldn't be where I am today without you both. Thanks to Kevin Smith for the keen editing eye. Thanks to Lori Flohaug for the excellent insight into some aspects of CPS; any inaccuracies are my fault, not hers. Thanks to Matt Iden for always having the time to read and tell me what's wrong and right in the story. Thanks to Richard Brown, Dori Pulley, Steven Konkoly, and Matt FitzSimmons—some of the best writers and people I know. Thanks to the Thomas & Mercer team for continuing to believe in the books. And thanks to all the readers who keep making what I do possible; I am forever in your debt.

ABOUT THE AUTHOR

Photo © 2019 Jade Hart

Joe Hart is the *Wall Street Journal* bestselling author of more than fifteen novels, including *Or Else*, *The River Is Dark*, *Obscura*, and *The Last Girl*. When not writing, he enjoys reading, exercising, exploring the great out doors, and watching movies with his family. For more information on his upcoming novels and access to his blog, visit www.joehartbooks.com.